RANDOM ACTS OF INIQUITY

HOLLY ANNA PALADIN MYSTERIES, BOOK 7

CHRISTY BARRITT

River Heights

COMPLETE BOOK LIST

Squeaky Clean Mysteries:

#14 Cold Case: Clean Sweep

While You Were Sweeping, A Riley Thomas Spinoff

The Sierra Files:

#1 Pounced

#2 Hunted

#3 Pranced

#4 Rattled

#5 Caged (coming soon)

The Gabby St. Claire Diaries (a Tween Mystery series):

The Curtain Call Caper

The Disappearing Dog Dilemma

The Bungled Bike Burglaries

The Worst Detective Ever

#1 Ready to Fumble

#2 Reign of Error

#3 Safety in Blunders

#4 Join the Flub

#5 Blooper Freak

#6 Flaw Abiding Citizen

#7 Gaffe Out Loud

#8 Joke and Dagger (coming soon)

Raven Remington

Relentless 1

Relentless 2 (coming soon)

Holly Anna Paladin Mysteries:

#1 Random Acts of Murder

#2 Random Acts of Deceit

#2.5 Random Acts of Scrooge

#3 Random Acts of Malice

#4 Random Acts of Greed

#5 Random Acts of Fraud

#6 Random Acts of Outrage

#7 Random Acts of Iniquity

Lantern Beach Mysteries

#1 Hidden Currents

#2 Flood Watch

#3 Storm Surge

#4 Dangerous Waters

#5 Perilous Riptide

#6 Deadly Undertow

Lantern Beach Romantic Suspense

Tides of Deception

Shadow of Intrigue

Storm of Doubt

Lantern Beach P.D.

On the Lookout

Attempt to Locate

First Degree Murder

Dead on Arrival

Plan of Action (coming in May)

Carolina Moon Series
Home Before Dark
Gone By Dark
Wait Until Dark
Light the Dark
Taken By Dark

Suburban Sleuth Mysteries:
Death of the Couch Potato's Wife

Fog Lake Suspense:
Edge of Peril
Margin of Error

Cape Thomas Series:
Dubiosity
Disillusioned
Distorted

Standalone Romantic Mystery:
The Good Girl

Suspense:
Imperfect
The Wrecking

Standalone Romantic-Suspense:
Keeping Guard
The Last Target
Race Against Time
Ricochet
Key Witness
Lifeline
High-Stakes Holiday Reunion
Desperate Measures
Hidden Agenda
Mountain Hideaway
Dark Harbor
Shadow of Suspicion
The Baby Assignment
The Cradle Conspiracy

Nonfiction:
Characters in the Kitchen
Changed: True Stories of Finding God through Christian Music (out of print)
The Novel in Me: The Beginner's Guide to Writing and Publishing a Novel (out of print)

CHAPTER ONE

AN ACHE JOSTLED me from a total blackout state. An ache in my head.

Dull pain pounded. Pounded. Pounded, almost like someone had taken a hammer to my skull and continuously swung it.

Something was wrong. Really wrong.

Think, Holly. What happened? Where are you?

Using all of my willpower, I forced my eyes open. My vision blurred. More pain shot through me until I squeezed my eyes shut again. A few minutes later, the pain subsided enough for me to think.

Focus on what you can comprehend, even with your eyes closed. What do you feel?

I moved my fingers—just barely, though. Something soft pillowed beneath my palms. Maybe a blanket? Sheets?

Maybe I'd had a medical emergency. Could I be at the hospital, blacked out right now? In a coma? Was this what it would feel like?

It definitely didn't smell like a hospital, and I doubted hospitals had sheets this soft. Plus, I was on my belly, and it was quiet. Too quiet. A hospital would be filled with beeps and voices in the background.

Okay, what else? What do you hear, Holly? Use your senses.

I swallowed hard, trying to focus. But I heard nothing, only the pounding in my head. *Bam. Bam. Bam.*

The pain enveloped me until I let out a cry.

I was a social worker by trade, but I temporarily worked for my brother who was a state senator. I was twenty-nine. Single. A foster mom. I wasn't the kind of person who went clubbing or drank unmonitored drinks or who blacked out and had no sense of place.

I tried to move my arm, but my limbs felt heavy, like weights had been tied around them.

I'd been drugged, I realized. It was the only thing that made sense. But I had no recollection of why I might be drugged or if a doctor or someone else had put me in this state.

Panic surged through me again.

Pull yourself together and open your eyes. You can do it. You have to do it. Maybe your family is all standing around you, waiting for this very moment when you show you're awake.

I drew in several more deep breaths. I didn't want to freak out. In order to obey my mental orders, I needed to focus.

On the count of three, I tried to force open my eyes again. They barely slit open this time, allowing me to see a sliver of my environment. Everything was blurry. My surroundings were bright. So bright it hurt my eyes. Caused my eyelids to close like floodgates trying to stop an impending disaster.

The darkness swallowed me again.

Okay, so it was bright around me? Did that mean I was outside?

My instincts told me no. The temperature seemed too consistent, too perfect. I must be inside a room with a light on.

I drew in another breath, this one not as shaky. Maybe I was finally gaining some control. What I knew was this: I lay on a soft fabric in a bright, climate-controlled area. That was *something*.

Dear Lord, help me. What's going on?

My gut told me something was majorly wrong. My instincts were poised in anticipation of danger. The last thing I remembered was . . .

I flexed my fingers beneath me again.

What was the last thing I remembered? That was right. I'd been at my house. In the evening. My foster daughter, Sarah, was with her biological mom for the week on a family trip. Drew Williams, my ex-boyfriend, was out of town at a conference. My mom had remarried and was on her honeymoon in the Caribbean.

I'd been baking cookies when . . . I heard someone at the door.

My body stiffened as the memories slowly trickled to the forefront of my thoughts, feeling like a poison spreading over my mind.

My heart pulsed more quickly.

That was right. Someone had rang the bell. I'd gone to answer it and . . .

My head pounded again. Harder. And harder until I flinched.

What had happened next?

I tried to form a clearer picture in my mind. But maybe some kind of internal self-preservation wouldn't allow the facts to come into focus. Maybe the memories were too awful for me to recall, awful enough that blacking out seemed a better option.

A sickly feeling roiled in my gut.

I had to remember what had happened, whether I wanted to or not.

I drew in a deep breath, trying to regain control of . . . something. Anything.

In an instant, I flashed back in time. My doorbell had rung. I'd gone to answer it. My last batch of cookies had just come out of the oven, and the heavenly scent of snickerdoodles drifted through the house.

Chase, I remembered. Chase Dexter.

He was supposed to stop by. Chase was my high school crush, a Cincinnati detective, a former professional football player, a Chris Hemsworth lookalike, and the man who had broken my heart.

Despite that, we'd remained friends.

Chase had said he would drop off some flyers about a new youth initiative the police department was doing. I worked with inner city youth, and I was going to try to spread the word.

But Chase hadn't been at my door when I'd opened it.

I squeezed my eyes together as the nausea in my gut grew stronger.

A strange man had been at my door, I remembered. A man in a mask. The disguise had featured rosy cheeks. A big fake grin. White skin like a porcelain doll. A creepy porcelain doll.

I'd screamed.

Stepped back.

Tried to shut the door. But it had been too late. The man grabbed me. Shoved something over my mouth and nose. Something with a sweet scent.

And now I was here. I didn't remember anything after that.

A sob escaped from somewhere deep inside. What had he done to me? Terror swept through my bones, causing an earthquake-like tremor through my body.

My fingers rubbed the buttery-soft fabric beneath me

again. I desperately needed something to keep me grounded, to remind me I was still alive. There was still hope . . . right?

Images began to pummel me. Possibilities of what had happened. Anxiety gripped my thoughts.

Don't let anxiety win.

I'd just gone to a conference on that subject as part of my certification as a social worker. That was one of the things they'd talked about—controlling anxiety before it spiraled. I needed to apply that advice now.

I needed to see for myself where I was. I could do this. I could take charge of my floundering emotions.

I moaned as I turned. I was definitely lying down. Maybe on a bed. Maybe on the floor on a blanket. I wasn't sure.

The man must have drugged me with more than whatever had been on the cloth he'd put over my face. That would explain the ache in my head, my blurry vision, and the general groggy feeling that lingered. Eventually, the effects would wear off.

More anxiety churned inside me at the possibility of opening my eyes again. I knew I had to do it, but I dreaded the dizziness that would come, followed by pain and the disoriented feeling.

I swallowed hard and forced my eyes open.

A room slowly came into focus.

A bedroom.

I was on a bed, I realized. A twin bed. With a pink bedspread. A white dresser. Lacy curtains.

Everything spun again, and I squeezed my eyes shut.

Where in the world was I? In a little girl's room? It made no sense.

My head was heavy. So heavy.

I was so tired of fighting the exhaustion that pressed at me.

Sleep beckoned me. Fought for my attention. Begged me to surrender.

And, against my better instincts, I let sleep win.

———

MY EYES JERKED open with a start.

The pink, lacy bedroom came into sight again. My lungs deflated only briefly before seizing with fright.

That was right. I'd been drugged and left here by the strange man who'd come to my door wearing a creepy mask. I had no idea where I was, how long I'd been here, or if anyone knew I was gone.

My head still hurt, but not as bad. Everything wasn't as blurry. The drugs were wearing off.

But I was far, far from being out of the woods.

With a groan, I pushed myself up.

Just as I remembered, I was lying on the princess-style bed in a strange room. I paused until everything around me stopped spinning. Every limb trembled uncontrollably.

The drugs? Terror? Probably both.

Drawing up my knees, I glanced down and blanched. What was I wearing? I had on a dress. I liked dresses, especially 1950s-style outfits.

But I'd never seen this dress before. It was yellow with a tight waist, a billowing skirt, and fitted top. Were those . . . I stared at my legs. Pantyhose? I was also wearing pantyhose and some rounded-toe heels.

My heart beat harder.

Those definitely weren't mine.

Tears pressed my eyes as the sickly feeling in my stomach continued to grow.

Whatever was going on here . . . it terrified me.

I'd been dressed up, almost like a doll. This had not been what I was wearing earlier. No, as I'd lounged at home, I'd been wearing my favorite pajama bottoms—the ones that were white and decorated with watermelon slices—along with a comfy red shirt.

I needed to move. Every minute counted right now. I could be missing my opportunity to get away.

Drawing on all my strength, I swung my legs to the floor. I nearly stumbled as I stood. My muscles felt like rubber. I caught myself on the edge of the bed and waited just a moment until I felt steady.

I spotted a door in the distance. My way out. I darted toward it.

I grabbed the knob and twisted.

It was locked.

An airy cry escaped from me.

I should have known.

I turned and, leaning against the door to remain steady, I glanced at the rest of the room.

The windows. I needed to check the windows. See if they were locked or if I could break them.

I sprinted across the room, nearly stumbling but catching myself. I jerked the heavy curtain aside.

My heart sank when I saw what was on the other side.

Wooden boards had been nailed on the outside covering the glass.

I wasn't getting out of this room, I realized. Someone had ensured that.

I pushed down another round of panic and sagged against the bed.

If only I could remember what had happened during my black hours. Who might have done this. Why.

Nothing made sense right now.

Don't panic, Holly. Think proactively. Think like a survivor, not a victim.

I needed to take a closer look at my surroundings. See if there was anything I could use to aid my escape or to protect myself. That's what Chase would tell me. He was a police detective, so he should know.

At the thought of him, my chin trembled. Faces of all my loved ones flashed through my mind, my heart.

Did they know I'd been abducted? Were they worried? Did they know how much I loved them?

I couldn't think about that now. The thought of them worrying crippled me.

Solutions, Holly. Solutions.

With a push, I propelled myself from the bed. I grabbed the handle on one of the dresser drawers. I tugged but nothing happened. What?

I tugged harder.

Still nothing.

I tried the next drawer. It was also locked.

They all were.

What? All of this . . . it was no accident. It had been planned. Carefully executed.

I straightened and heaved in a shaky breath.

Okay, that hadn't worked. But I needed to keep thinking, keep searching. I glanced around.

There was nothing else in the room. No lamps. No other doors—not even a closet. No knickknacks. Only lacy pillows and curtains.

I rushed back toward the door and rattled the knob again.

Just as last time, it didn't budge.

I knelt and examined the handle. Two screws held it in place. If I could get them out, maybe I could take the knob off.

My dad had been a locksmith and had taught me a few tricks of the trade.

I jammed my index finger into the edge of the screw. As I tried to turn it, my fingernail ripped.

I jerked my hand back and shook out the pain. That hadn't felt good. I needed something stronger than my fingernail to twist this screw out.

I leaned back, trying to sort my thoughts. My head pulsed again, and my mouth felt unnaturally dry. I needed water. How long would I last in here? Twenty or so days with no food, but only a few days with no water? That wasn't comforting.

I *had* to get out of this room.

I glanced back at the dresser. The drawers had brassy handles. If I could leverage one from its holder and pull it out . . .

It was worth a shot.

I crawled over to examine it. Grabbing the golden metal, I pushed and pulled until finally one of the handles came off. A surge of victory rushed through me.

I stared at the end of the metal piece. It just might be flat enough to work.

I crawled back to the door. My hands still trembled as I rose on my knees and used the edge of the handle to catch the screw. I sucked in a breath. It fit.

I turned the handle like a crank, adjusting it as I worked to loosen the doorknob. After a few minutes, the screw fell to the ground.

Moisture pressed at my eyes as hope rose.

Maybe this would work. Maybe I'd get out of here.

Or Chase would find me.

Or Drew.

Their two images clashed in my mind.

Drew who wanted forever. Chase who steered away from commitment.

Two men who were day and night.

One whom my heart adored. The other who logically made sense.

Since the two had come into my life, I'd been conflicted.

Now, all I wanted was to see them. To feel strong arms around me. To listen to someone telling me everything would be okay.

I worked the other screw until it also fell out. Then I began to dissect the door knob. Piece by piece, I pulled the mechanism from the door until a hole was left there.

I swallowed back a sob of relief.

With caution, I opened the door. I kept the brassy drawer pull in my hand, prepared to use the edge as a weapon if I had to.

I scanned the space in front of me. I appeared to be in a house. In a bedroom at the end of a long hallway. A living room and kitchen probably waited on the other end.

Everything appeared clean and neat. Pictures of flowers hung on the walls. An artificial fern sat in the corner. The peaceful image clashed with the truth until I felt nauseated.

As I stepped onto the carpeted hallway, a deep voice cut through the air.

"Holly Anna Paladin."

I froze and goosebumps climbed across my skin. Where had that voice come from?

This was far from over. I wouldn't be escaping.

No, I had a feeling the worst was yet to come.

My head swam at the thought.

CHAPTER TWO

I SWUNG MY GAZE AROUND, desperately looking for the source of the voice.

I saw no one. Only a dim hallway. A few doors. The great unknown beyond that.

Where had that voice come from? It had sounded right on top of me.

"Good job getting out of the room, Holly," the man said. "I underestimated you."

I jerked my gaze up and saw a tiny speaker had been mounted in the corner of the ceiling, along with a camera.

Whoever my captor was, he was hiding behind those devices. Realizing that brought a surge of anger through me. Coward. Yet my anger did nothing to diffuse my fear.

I glanced up at the camera. My voice shook as I asked, "Who are you?"

"It doesn't matter." The man's voice sounded even and controlled, like he had no qualms about doing this. "Walk down the hallway."

I stared down the dim hallway, my mind racing. I imagined someone jumping out or other horrors that might await. This pink bedroom wasn't exactly safe, but at least it was familiar.

"Why?"

"Because I told you to!" His voice intensified. "Now move."

Was that voice familiar? I didn't think so.

I swallowed hard, some kind of fight rising in me. The man wasn't here. What was he going to do to me? In his cowardice, could I find some courage?

"What if I don't?" I rubbed my neck, instantly second-guessing my words.

He said nothing for a minute. "You're more stubborn than I thought you'd be. But that's not going to work. Now, act like a good, submissive woman and follow my directions. Am I clear?"

The man wasn't playing. I felt certain I'd face consequences if I didn't listen. I didn't know what kind, especially if he wasn't right here. But, for all I knew, he could be in the next room.

"Yes," I said.

"Yes, sir," he corrected.

My throat burned, but I said, "Yes, sir."

Nausea roiled in my stomach. I was dressed like a 1950s housewife, trapped in an old-style house, and he'd used the word submissive. I saw a pattern emerging, but I wasn't ready to acknowledge what it all might mean.

"Good girl. Start moving. Now."

My legs trembled as I took the first step. My hand—the one without my weapon—skimmed the wall. My gait still felt unsteady.

I studied the ceiling above me. Were there more cameras? More speakers so the man could communicate? I had a feeling he was watching my every move.

There was so much I didn't know—and that terrified me.

"Stop," the man said.

I froze at the end of the hallway. As I did, the lights came on in front of me, revealing a retro-style kitchen. Normally, I would love a place like this with its historic charm.

All the appliances were old school and teal. The floor was checkered black and white. The countertops appeared to be a black Formica lined with chrome trim. I felt like I'd stepped back in time

This time, I wanted out.

"There's a menu on the counter. Fix everything listed. Wear the apron that was left for you on the counter. Don't ask questions. Women are meant to be seen, not heard."

I flinched at the voice. In the corner of the kitchen, I spotted another camera and speaker.

I had no idea what this man's endgame was . . . but the possibilities terrified me.

He was making me into a 1950s housewife, wasn't he?

I shuddered.

"You need to get to work. Now. Do I make myself clear?"

I swallowed hard and stepped into the kitchen. As I did, I straightened the skirt of my unfamiliar yellow dress. "Yes . . . sir."

On the kitchen counter, I found a note. *Chicken pot pie. Lemon crème pie. A garden salad with homemade ranch dressing. Sweet tea. Dinner for two will be served at 5:30.*

5:30?

I glanced around, looking for the time.

A clock on the wall said it was 4:00 now. Did that mean I'd been missing all night and all day?

The pit in my stomach grew deeper as I realized how many hours I couldn't recall.

What exactly would happen at 5:30? Would my captor arrive? Would he eat?

And then what?

A gasp escaped from my lips.

I didn't want to think about it. Instead, I pulled on

the ruffled white apron and tied it around my waist. I needed to get started.

MY HANDS TREMBLED as I began preparing dinner. I took a quick break, long enough to smooth my hair and take a sip of water. I glanced at the camera from the corner of my eye, certain my captor was watching my every move. Then I turned back to my prep area, knowing I had to be mindful of the time.

As I peeled a potato, I glanced over at the butcher block full of knives. Could I grab one? Use it as a weapon if necessary?

I kept that idea in the back of my mind. I couldn't afford to let my guard down right now. I had to be mindful of the things around me and keep my eyes wide open. It was the only way I was going to get out of this situation.

I knew that behind me, there was a living room with a low-profile blue couch. Just beyond a half wall to my left, I spotted a dining room table with a glossy teal top edged with chrome sides and legs. Matching glossy, padded chairs sat around it.

There were windows there. No doubt they were covered in wood behind the curtains.

I swallowed hard and continued to work. The pot pie, prepared in a large cast iron skillet, went into the oven. The lemon pie went into the fridge. I started on the salad and glanced at the time again.

I still had thirty minutes left.

Thirty minutes to think of a way out.

My hands shook as I took a glass bottle of buttermilk from the fridge and whisked it with some mayonnaise, sour cream, and herbs to make ranch dressing. I poured it into a glass container with a small spout, put the top on it, and stepped back.

Finally, everything was done—for now. The chicken pot pie had to finish baking. The lemon pie had to cool. I needed to set the table.

I grabbed some silverware and scurried into the dining room. As I stepped into the room, I glanced around. My breaths were entirely too shallow. At this rate, I'd pass out. Despite that, I set the utensils at the proper seats.

I'd done this many times for my family and friends. I loved hospitality. I loved taking care of people. Making them feel at home. But not like this. Not under duress. Not because I was forced to do so.

My stomach twisted harder, tighter.

I wondered about my family again. Did they miss me? Realize I was gone?

How about Jamie? I was supposed to meet my best friend for lunch. When I didn't show up, would she be worried?

And then there was Drew . . . I knew he would do

everything in his power to find me—after he realized I was missing. But he was out of town, and we didn't talk every day anymore since we'd broken up about a month ago.

Speaking of which, I needed to have him over for dinner when he returned home. I'd been thinking about it for a while now. Would I ever have the chance to say the things I needed to say?

Then there was Chase . . . Chase.

I straightened a placemat on the table. My heart pounded in my chest as I thought about him. He'd already lost so much in his life. Even though I knew I wasn't that important to him, how would he handle another loss? Would it break him? Or would he truly not care?

I pressed my fingertips into the table as my thoughts raced.

I needed to get out of here. I needed to see the people I cared about. More than anything, I wanted to take care of them. That's who I was. A nurturer. I couldn't have them worried about me now.

As I double-checked the place settings, I glanced at the front door. I could make a run for it.

But I knew it was probably locked up tight.

Something hummed above me. I looked up and saw that the camera had moved and fully faced me now.

The man was still watching me. If I made one wrong move, he'd make me pay. I was sure of it.

The timer dinged in the kitchen, and I nearly jumped out of my skin. I hurried into the room and grabbed an oven mitt. Carefully, I pulled the cast iron pan from the oven. The casserole smelled heavenly, and my stomach grumbled.

What would happen next? I'd cooked the food for the man. Would he come to get it?

Another crush of anxiety rose in me.

"Why is this happening?" I whispered, looking at the ceiling, to God.

His voice wasn't the one who responded.

"Good job on preparing dinner, Holly. Step away from the kitchen counter and stand near the sink. And don't even think about making any sudden moves or grabbing one of those knives from the butcher block."

The trembles started back in my hands as I did as he said. I gave one last look at the camera, trying to anticipate his next move.

A click sounded in the distance. It sounded like a door opening.

My throat went dry. The man was here. I was certain of it.

Footsteps came toward me. Closer. Closer.

The skin on my neck crawled as I braced myself for whatever might come. I preferred being alone with cameras to seeing this man face-to-face.

CHAPTER THREE

A MAN WEARING the same creepy mask stepped into the kitchen. A fitted suit stretched across his lean frame, and he held a briefcase. But I couldn't see his true expression or what he really looked like.

That terrified me.

He placed his briefcase on the floor and paced closer. "Is dinner ready?"

My voice trembled as I said, "Yes, sir."

"Good girl. I hope it's hot. I had a long, hard day at work, and I don't want any drama. A man deserves to relax after work, don't you think?"

"Of course."

"I'll watch you as you serve dinner."

"Whatever makes you happy." I was playing along, but doing so left a sick feeling in my stomach. I pulled two plates from the cabinet and set them on the counter before reaching for a serving spoon for the chicken pot pie.

The man stepped closer as I stood at the stove. His hands went to my waist, and he rested them there, like they belonged.

"Good job, honey." His hot breath hit my ear.

Bile rose in me.

Feeling him touch me. Feeling his breath on me . . . it ignited something in me.

I had to think defensively. I had to fight back. It was the only thing that made sense.

I stuck the spoon into the crispy bread atop the casserole. With my other hand, I reached for the handle of the pan.

As I did, an idea hit me. It was risky. Really risky. Too risky.

But what choice did I have?

I grabbed the pan from the stove with both hands, turned it, and swung it toward the man's head.

It collided with his mask. I heard an *ump*. Then a thud.

I glanced around. The man lay on the floor. Chicken pot pie had splattered around his head.

I couldn't look at him long. I had to get out of here.

Bending down, I reached into his pocket.

Keys. There were keys there.

I grabbed them and dashed toward the door. I gripped the knob, but it was locked, as I'd suspected.

I took the keys and began jamming them into the mechanism. Finally, one fit.

I glanced behind me, breathless as I expected to see the man appear in the doorway.

He didn't.

Quickly, I turned the key. Twisted the handle. Scrambled outside.

I squinted against the sunlight and briefly surveyed my surroundings.

I was in a neighborhood, it appeared. A normal, all-American-looking neighborhood.

I started forward, desperate to run, but my legs wobbled. Quickly, I pulled off my heels and tossed them over my shoulder. I'd take my chances barefoot.

I dashed down the walkway, the driveway, to the sidewalk in front of the house. I didn't look back. Didn't want to see if the man was chasing me. If he'd come to from his unconscious state.

Still feeling out of sorts, I sprinted to the house next door and pounded on the door. Anxiety crawled across my skin as I waited, knowing I was on borrowed time. I couldn't stay here long.

Please, answer!

But I heard nothing. No movement. No signs of life.

I had to move. Get as far away from that man as possible.

I darted across the lawn, away from the house of horrors. More details of the neighborhood around me processed in my mind. Newer, craftsman style homes built to replicate the charm of times past surrounded me. No cars were in the driveways. Sod lay across the lawns, and sapling-sized trees had been planted.

The street was deserted. Where was everyone? The vast emptiness of the neighborhood left me with an eerie feeling.

A sound in the distance caught my ear. Was that . . . the zoom of traffic? Could there be a highway nearby?

My heart skipped a beat. Where there was a highway, there were people.

I needed people. I needed a safe place to call the police.

I rounded the corner onto another street. A gas station appeared in the distance.

My heart lifted. I had to make it there. Cars were in the parking lot. Unlike this neighborhood, that business wasn't deserted.

I glanced over my shoulder.

I still didn't see the man.

Finally, I reached the front door of the gas station and threw it open. The customers inside stopped and stared at me.

"Help." I collapsed on the dirty floor near the entrance. "I need help."

I SAT in a desk chair in the office of the gas station. Like a child, I pulled my knees to my chest and nibbled on my fingernails. I felt like I was here in this room yet separate from my body. I felt like I should panic, but instead I felt a wave of numbness. I knew what had just happened, yet it didn't seem real.

The gas station manager—who was probably younger than I was—lingered near the doorway, appearing nervous as he paced, occasionally glancing at me.

He obviously didn't know what to say. And I didn't need him to say anything. There was nothing that could be said. Besides, he probably thought I was either high or off my meds. That seemed more plausible than the truth.

The manager's head jerked up, and he took a step toward someone. I lowered my legs to the floor, my lungs frozen. Someone was finally here. Who?

A moment later, Chase Dexter appeared.

Tall, broad, brooding. Button-up shirt with sleeves rolled to his elbows. Blond hair disheveled. Clean shaven. The most handsome man I'd ever seen.

Suddenly our history didn't matter. How he'd broken my heart. How he couldn't commit.

I flew into his arms. He gathered me there and held me close. One of his hands cradled my head and the other tightened around my waist.

"Holly," he whispered into my hair. "I can't tell you what the past few hours have been like."

Tears flowed down my cheeks. I didn't try to stop them. I sobbed into Chase's chest, and Chase let me.

It wasn't until I stepped back that he took my face into his hands and examined my features. "Are you okay?"

I didn't know how to answer that, so I shrugged and felt the tears pressing at my eyes again.

Someone else entered the room and nodded to the manager as he left. Chase stepped back—but only slightly. He was still close enough to hold my arm, to catch me if I fell.

"This is Detective Wilson," Chase said. "He's going to take lead on this case. I wish I could, but I'm too close to it."

I quickly observed the slight man with glasses and a receding hairline. He was Chase's opposite, just based on appearances, at least, and probably nearing retirement—in his mid-fifties, I'd guess. He pushed something around in his mouth—a mint maybe.

The detective paused in the door, a compassionate look in his eyes as he addressed me. "Ms. Paladin, as Detective Dexter said, I'm Detective Wilson. Can you tell me what happened? Do you feel up to it?"

Did I? Not really? But I knew time was of the essence right now, and I would push past my dread if it meant catching this guy. "Yes . . . yes, I can do that."

Chase led me back to the seat behind the desk and lowered me there. Then he stood beside me like a guard as Detective Wilson took a seat across from me after closing the door.

"I guess I should just start at the beginning . . ." I drew in a shaky breath. Then I told them what I'd gone through. All the details. The horror. The things that didn't make sense.

"Can you tell me where you were held captive?" Detective Wilson asked.

"I . . . I might be able to find it. But . . . I . . . I can't go in." Panic swarmed in me at the thought of that retro kitchen. The pink bedroom. The chrome edged furniture of the dining room.

I couldn't face that place. I couldn't . . .

"We won't ask you to do that," Detective Wilson said quietly. "We just need to know where this took place."

I nodded resolutely, determined to be strong, even though I wanted to crumble. "I'll show you."

Chase's hand pressed on my shoulder. "I'll go with her."

Relief filled me. I wouldn't have to face this alone.

Thank God for friends.

CHAPTER FOUR

CHASE TOOK my hand into his as we sat together in the back seat of Detective Wilson's car. I craved human connection to keep me grounded and to remind me this wasn't a dream. For that reason, I squeezed Chase's fingers, never wanting to let go.

My stomach churned as I thought about seeing the house again. Would I recognize it? I thought I would but . . . I'd fled so quickly. My only goal had been to get away.

As we pulled into the neighborhood, the same eeriness from earlier washed over me. What was wrong with this community? Why did it feel more like a movie set than a place where people lived?

From the safety of the car, I observed the streets again. The houses, just as I remembered, looked old-school Americana with their porches and craftsman style. They weren't as large as most of the new homes being built. Fresh asphalt covered the street, and dirty tire tracks stretched down the middle.

"Where are we?" I asked, realizing I had no idea how far from home I was.

"We're on the north side of Cincinnati."

I blanched. That was a good forty minutes from my house near downtown. But it made sense. Lots of new neighborhoods were being developed in this area.

Detective Wilson slowed as we reached the first street. Dread built in me as we got closer and closer to the house of horror.

"Turn here," I muttered.

The detective followed my direction.

I could do this, I told myself. I could face the place I left behind.

This still seemed like a nightmare I'd woken up from. But it wasn't. As I glanced down at my dress, at the torn panty hose over my legs, I knew with certainty the events that had played out had really happened.

"Where next?" Wilson picked up a plastic box of orange Tic Tacs and guzzled a few into his mouth.

"Turn left up here. The house should be on the right, about eight lots down."

Chase squeezed my hand tighter, as if sensing my rising anxiety.

"Anything you remember about the house that

might help us identify it?" Wilson's voice still sounded gentle and prodding, and I appreciated his sensitivity.

I closed my eyes and tried to remember any details. "The windows are all covered with wood . . . I'm not sure what else."

The detective slowed. My eyes searched each house we passed. They were practically cookie cutter images of each other. Which house was it?

My head pounded as pressure pushed in on me. I had to be on my A game. We had to catch this guy.

"It's okay, Holly," Chase murmured. "Take your time."

I stared at the houses and tried to remember the color of the front door. Was it yellow? Or red?

I had no idea.

"They're all blending together." I shook my head. "I think I left the door open. But the man could have closed it."

"Was there a car in the driveway?" Wilson asked.

"No, I don't think there was. Maybe it was in the garage? This whole neighborhood kind of seems empty."

"It's just been built," Chase said. "Most of these homes aren't ready to be occupied. There have been some financial struggles, if I remember correctly."

"That's right," Wilson said. "Some investors have pulled out, and things have been put on hold until the developer works out his issues."

Everything made a little more sense then. Why there were no cars. Why no one was home.

But my house had definitely been decorated. Someone had started to move in.

"We're about at eight houses." Detective Wilson rolled the car to a stop.

I stared at each of the homes but shook my head. I had no idea which one I'd been in. I kept praying for something to stir a memory.

"That one has wood over the windows." My heart raced as I pointed to one.

"Several homes in this area have boarded-up windows," Chase said quietly. "There have been some break-ins in this neighborhood lately. Thieves have been shattering the windows to get inside."

My heart sank. I suppose that made sense.

"Shoes," I muttered. "I pulled off my shoes so I could run faster. I tossed them on the porch. The man could have grabbed them but—"

"How about this? I'll park here and check the porch for shoes. I'll check all the doors. See if any are ajar." Detective Wilson glanced at me. "Does that work?"

I nodded and clung to Chase's hand. I was glad no one forced me to see the house for myself.

Every time I closed my eyes, I remembered the bedroom. The retro kitchen. Seeing the man in the mask.

A shudder snaked through me.

I watched as Wilson climbed out of the car. Several

other police cruisers pulled up in the area, and a few officers began pacing the sidewalks, waiting for instructions.

Wilson sauntered to the house beside us. Tried to open the door. It appeared to be locked.

I just watched. I needed to see what he would figure out. I needed answers. I needed for this to be over.

Please, Lord.

He checked three more houses.

Nothing.

The hollow pit in my stomach grew, and my head wobbled again.

"So you never saw this guy's face?" Chase turned toward me, seeming to sense my weakening state.

"Just his mask. It made his face look like . . ." I trembled. "A porcelain doll. When I knocked him out, I probably should have removed it so I could see what he looked like . . ."

"You did the right thing by running as fast as you could."

But had I? If I had looked under the mask, I could identify this man right now. My choice could mean the difference in this guy getting away . . . or me.

Detective Wilson came back to the car and opened the door. "All the houses are locked up tight and there are no shoes in sight. Anything else you might remember that would give us a clue, Ms. Paladin? Anything will help."

I closed my eyes, trying to think. What was I missing? I couldn't remember anything specific that made this home stand out.

There had to be something, though.

As I glanced down at my skirt, I saw a stain there. I sucked in a breath. Some of my chicken pot pie had gotten on me when I swung the cast iron skillet. "I know this might sound crazy, but look for chicken pot pie. Peas. Carrots. Chicken. Some got on my skirt, and it could have fallen off as I ran."

Wilson stared at me a minute before nodding slowly, like he didn't know if I was joking or not. "Let me check it out."

As Wilson left, Chase pulled me toward him, and I rested my head against his thick chest.

I hoped they found the right house. I hoped they found the man responsible for this. But I wondered if I was hoping too much.

Wilson knelt on one of the porches, looking at the cement beneath him. A moment later, he stood and nodded toward an officer in the distance. Three men swarmed the area.

My heart lifted. Was this the house? Had they found it?

One of the men used a battering ram to knock open the door, and the men flooded inside.

I watched, unable to say anything. I could hardly breathe. I only waited. Waited.

As I did, I glanced outside. Saw the sun still stood high in the sky. But . . . that made no sense. "Chase, what time is it?"

He glanced at his watch. "Eleven."

I blinked, certain I hadn't heard him correctly. "Eleven in the morning?"

"That's right. Why?"

I shook my head. My timeline was all discombobulated. I thought for sure it was closer to evening. "It's just that . . . the man told me to make dinner. I thought . . . I thought more time had passed."

"That is strange. It was like he was playing some kind of game with you."

Game was a strange way to put it. Games were supposed to be fun. I certainly hadn't had fun, but maybe my captor had been living out some kind of sick fantasy.

Finally, Wilson emerged and sauntered back over. He opened my door and leaned against the car as he peered down to address me. "We found it."

A lump formed in my chest as good news collided with bad news. Good: They'd found the right location. Bad: This could be the moment of reckoning.

"Anything?" I asked, my voice catching.

"No one is there. But we're going to scour the place for evidence. In the meantime, we need to get you to the hospital to be checked out—"

"I'm fine." I just wanted to go home. I didn't want to

draw this out. And, really, I was unharmed—just shaken.

Wilson almost appeared fatherly as he looked at me. "We don't know what kind of drug he gave you. We'll need to know, just in case there are any effects, and also for the official report, of course."

I nodded. His explanation made sense. My tox screen would serve as evidence when this went to court. Not if. *When.* "Okay then."

"I'll take her," Chase said. "Can one of the guys take me back to my car?"

"I'll get one of them to do that right now."

————

AFTER CHASE and I were dropped off at the gas station, Chase led me to his unmarked police sedan. He didn't start the engine. Instead, he turned to me and brushed my hair out of my face.

His blue eyes looked tender, and his motions were gentle. His presence reminded me of a Roman centurion guarding something precious.

I was honored that, at the moment, that precious commodity was me.

This was the first moment the two of us had really had alone, and I, for one, was relieved to be away from everyone else. Away from the pressure of curious eyes.

Away from strangers who tried to ascertain my mental state.

The October day was mild, so the temperature inside the car remained pleasant without any AC or heat. At least there was that to be thankful for.

"Holly," Chase murmured again, just as he had inside the office when he'd first seen me. The word was filled with so much affection.

I leaned into his touch, wishing I could pull myself together. I wasn't sure it was possible, though. My emotions went off like flashbangs inside me, each one making me flinch.

"I wasn't able to reach your mom," Chase said.

"She's in the Caribbean on her honeymoon, and she left her phone at home in the ultimate 'Do Not Disturb' effort."

"Honeymoon? She got married?"

"That's right. It was spontaneous, but she seems really happy." My dad had been gone for several years now. Then my mom had met Larry Truman, and the two seemed made for each other. No one in the family had been surprised when they went to the Justice of the Peace and were married.

"I'm happy for her."

"We all are." My thoughts shifted back to my family and friends. "Does anyone else know?"

Chase let out a breath. "I called Jamie, Ralph, and

Alex, and I texted Drew. I needed to make sure you weren't with any of them."

I could only imagine the panic they might be feeling. I should have called them right away so I could ease their worries. I'd wasted so much time. "I'm going to need to let them know I'm okay."

"I can do that for you. While the doctor checks you out."

I nodded, feeling like I'd been dropped into another world. I knew I was moving and talking, but it almost seemed like someone else was doing so for me. Someone who looked and sounded like me but who wasn't me.

"It's going to be a long day, Holly."

"I know."

"What are you thinking?" Chase dropped his hand, but his gaze was still focused solely on me.

"I can't stop reviewing everything that happened."

"Why don't you walk me through what happened again? Maybe it will help you sort things out."

I drew in a deep breath, trying to prepare myself to share the details again. "I can't stop thinking about when the man came into the house."

"What did he do?"

"He set his briefcase down and came toward me." I shivered. "I felt like I'd stepped into an episode of *Leave It to Beaver*. I mean, I woke up in this dress. I had to fix dinner, and it had to be ready by 5:30 . . ."

"He didn't . . ." Chase's voice caught, and he rubbed his lips together, as if the words wouldn't leave his mouth.

"He didn't touch me." Praise the Lord. But I glanced at my clothes. "Although, I don't know how I got into this dress."

Chase nodded, but I saw the emotion in his eyes. I saw the worry. The concern. The flash of relief.

"It sounds to me like this was someone who knew you, Holly. Who knew enough about you to know you love everything retro. Maybe he was obsessed with you and that's why he set you up in a scenario like this."

I shivered. "Maybe."

"Has there been anyone who's given you strange vibes lately? Maybe someone at work?"

I searched my thoughts. "Off the top of my head? No, I can't think of anyone."

"You still have time. Let's get you to the hospital."

I nodded. "Okay. Let's go."

I just wanted to get this over with.

CHAPTER FIVE

SIX HOURS LATER, Chase and I were back at my house. The doctor had examined me, given me some pain medication for my head injury—it was really just a big knot at the back of my skull—and run a tox screen. The police had taken my clothes as evidence and had given me some old sweat pants and a T-shirt instead.

During the process, Chase had stayed with me as much as he could. He'd even called my family and Jamie and had given them an update while I'd seen the doctor.

Throughout it all, I saw the pull of tension in his eyes. The desire to find answers versus the desire to protect me. He'd chosen to protect me, and I was grateful for that.

When the police had finished checking my home for

evidence, we were cleared to go back. Chase had insisted on staying with me. That was fine by me because I didn't want to be alone right now. I didn't want to face my house by myself. I couldn't stop picturing opening my door and seeing that man there.

Now, Chase's hand rested on my back as we stood at my front door. Darkness had fallen around us, and the day had been long. Really long.

Chase took the keys from my trembling hands and inserted them into the front door lock. I should be finding comfort in my little white bungalow with its wide porch and repurposed furnishings. The place, with its lovely view of the city, was normally my haven.

Quietly, he unlocked the door for me and led me inside.

I shuddered as I stepped through the door.

This was where it had all started less than twenty-four hours ago. I was thankful the ordeal hadn't lasted longer. But it had lasted long enough.

Chase took the Chinese food we'd picked up on the way and placed it on my kitchen table. I didn't tell him I wasn't hungry, and I was sure he was going to insist that I needed to eat. And I probably did.

I was feeling lightheaded and weak. The doctor said I might have some PTSD symptoms after what had happened. I'd majored in social work and counseling, so I knew all about trauma and what it did to the brain.

I was just glad that Sarah wasn't here right now.

Though I missed my foster daughter, the last thing she needed was to see me in this state. She'd been through enough distress in her life.

In fact, I'd requested no one see me tonight. Right now, I just needed to recover.

Chase paused by the table, the sleeves to his button-up shirt still rolled up to his elbows. He told me he'd taken the rest of the day off work and insisted that arguing with him about it would do no good.

"You don't have to eat if you don't want to," he said as he opened a carton of food and steam rose from it.

I blinked, unsure if I'd heard him correctly. I stared at the General Tso's Chicken in front of me, my stomach churning. Its spicy scent usually made my stomach growl. Right now, however, the dish had no appeal.

I pushed away my empty paper plate. "Good, because I think I might puke."

"Do you mind if I eat?"

"Not at all."

I watched as he put some fried rice and beef with broccoli on his plate. As he did so, I took a sip of my water. Every time I closed my eyes, flashbacks hit me.

Flashbacks of waking up in the strange room. Flashbacks of the fear caused by such vast uncertainty. Flashbacks of hearing the man walk into the house and not knowing what would happen next.

"Any updates from Wilson?" I forced my thoughts back to the present.

"They didn't find much evidence in the house that will tell us who this man was. The kitchen had been cleaned up before we arrived. I think the biggest clue will be if we can trace anything using the cameras that were all over the place."

I shivered as I remembered them. "Right. This had been set up for a while."

Chase stabbed a piece of broccoli. "You're right. It was like someone had been planning this. All the finishes in the home, the style . . . honestly, it gives me a cold chill when I think about it."

"Who owned the home?" Could that be the connection? Deep inside, I knew the man who'd abducted me was too smart for that, though. He'd meticulously planned this. No way would he overlook a detail like that.

"Officially? The developer owns the home. Wilson is still looking into it."

"The thing is . . . the house had flooring and furniture and appliances. Certainly someone had to see them being brought in. Someone had to install them."

"Wilson realizes that also. It will just take some time to talk to all the right people."

I frowned before standing and grabbing some of the snickerdoodle cookies I'd baked the day before. I set a plate of them on the table, just in case Chase wanted dessert. "I know. It all just seems surreal, Chase."

I crossed my arms and leaned back in my seat, swallowed by my thoughts. "I just can't stop thinking about this. This crime . . . it seems so random. When I answered the door, I fully expected it to be you last night."

Chase frowned and pushed his plate away, his food barely touched. "I must have shown up fifteen minutes after you were abducted."

I tried to picture it all playing out. "How did the house look when you got here?"

"Normal. Nothing looked out of the ordinary. The door was closed, and nothing was askew."

"When did you realize something was wrong?"

"I know you're a woman of your word. But I got a text from you, saying that you'd made other plans. That didn't sound like you."

"A text from me? I didn't send a text." And then the truth hit me. "The man must have my phone."

"He must." Chase picked up his fork again but only picked at his food. "I'll make sure Wilson tracks your cell location, just in case the man still has it."

"How did you know I was gone then?"

"Something just didn't feel right. I tried to brush it off. I patrolled by your house a couple times, thinking you might come home. You didn't. I started to get worried. I waited until this morning to call Ralph and Alex and to text Drew. They hadn't heard from you. Finally, I got up with Jamie, and she had no idea where you might be. That's when I knew something was truly wrong."

Absently, I picked up a cookie and began to nibble on it. It wasn't because I was hungry. I just wanted something to occupy myself with. "I feel like I should know more, Chase. That I should be able to point the police in the right direction and help them find this guy."

"The truth is, it could have been random. It could have been someone who saw you while you were out and about and who became obsessed. There may not be a logical explanation."

"I really like logical explanations."

"We all do. Random crimes . . . somehow, they're more frightening because we never saw them coming. But we're still early in this investigation, Holly. Let's give this more time. The police will be working around the clock on this." Chase lowered his voice, all his attention on me.

I nodded. He was right, and I was too wound up right now to think clearly. So much had happened, and it would take a while to process.

Chase leaned back. "You look exhausted."

"I am." My head pounded. My pain medication might be making me tired as well.

"Why don't you go to bed?"

The thought of being alone . . . I didn't like it. It made me feel like I was back in that house again.

Trapped in that room. All alone.

Despite that, I stood. Chase followed my lead, his chair scraping across the floor.

"That's probably a good idea."

Chase stepped closer, his gaze serious. "If it's okay, I'd like to sleep on your couch tonight. At least until we have some answers."

Chase was afraid this guy would come back. At the thought of it, I shivered again.

"That would be fine," I finally said. "Although, I do have an extra bedroom . . ." I pointed behind me with my thumb.

"I'd feel better out here where I can monitor things better."

I nodded, my throat abnormally tight. "Okay then. If you don't mind . . . that would be great. I'll sleep a lot better."

I would. Having Chase here, I knew I'd have someone watching out for me.

"Then you head on to bed. I'll take care of everything out here. Don't worry about me."

"Pillow and extra blanket are in the hall closet."

"I'll find them. Goodnight, Holly."

My throat felt achy as I said, "Goodnight, Chase. Thank you for everything."

His eyes were warm as he peered down at me. "Anytime."

I squeezed his arm, hoping with that one motion I

could show my appreciation for everything he'd done.

———

EVERY TIME SLEEP FOUND ME, horrible memories slashed into my slumber.

A cold sweat covered my skin.

I fully expected to wake up and find myself back in that pink lacy bedroom. I expected to feel a strange dress on me. To feel my head pounding.

I squeezed my pillow as panic seized my muscles.

Finally, I pushed myself up in bed. My heart raced as I stared at the darkness around me. I waited for a shadow to move. To hear a faceless voice. For a reason to confirm my panic.

What if that man found me again? What if it happened when I least expected it?

Nausea roiled in me at the thought.

I jerked my gaze around my room, looking for movement.

I saw nothing.

But what if the man was here? What if he had eyes on me somehow? What if there was a camera planted within the safety of my private space?

I held my stomach as I lurched forward.

I could hardly breathe. My head began to pound again until I wanted to crawl out of my skin.

You can do this, Holly. You can get through this.

But tears pressed at my eyes.

I didn't feel at all like I could get through this. Instead, I wanted to bury myself under a blanket and stay there. Lock myself in a room where no one could get to me.

I'd been through a lot in my twenty-nine years, but I never remembered feeling like this. Feeling hopeless. Paralyzed with fright.

Pull yourself together, Holly.

My mental scolding did nothing.

Instead, I stared at the window. I waited to see movement in the shadows there. Waited to hear something scrape against the panes as the man tried to get inside again.

I pulled the blanket closer around me, but it did no good.

This blanket wouldn't protect me.

I had to get out of this room. What if I couldn't? What if the door was locked? If wood covered my windows?

Scrambling, I pulled a sweatshirt on over my T-shirt and yoga pants, then opened the door. I didn't even know where I was going or what I was doing.

I only knew I was losing my mind in that room. If I stayed one second longer . . . I might have a complete breakdown.

I padded down the hallway and paused in the living room.

Chase lay there on the couch, a blanket pulled around him and a pillow tucked under his head.

Chase . . . the man I'd loved for so long. The man I'd thought I was going to marry. The man to whom I'd given my first kiss.

Despite everything that had transpired between us, he was my safety. He always had been.

My feet seemed to take on a mind of their own. I walked toward him, staring at his sleeping figure.

Before I could question myself, I lay down beside him and tucked myself into the folds of his arms.

"What . . ." He stirred, his voice sleepy. "Holly?"

I didn't say anything. I just lay there in his arms, craving the security he brought. Craving human touch.

"Holly . . ."

"Just hold me," I whispered. "Please."

Finally, his muscles relaxed. He slipped his arm around my waist and pulled me closer.

I relished the feel of having him so near. Maybe I shouldn't. This wasn't like me. I didn't do stuff like this.

But I knew this was innocent. I wasn't making a move or trying to put anyone—including myself—into a bad situation.

No, I only wanted comfort in my panic. I was desperate for it. Desperate to not feel so alone right now. Was that a sin?

I didn't know.

I closed my eyes, eager for sleep. But before I drifted off, I felt Chase kiss the top of my head.

"I love you, Holly," he muttered.

My heart nearly froze.

Had I really heard those words? Or was I just dreaming?

I wasn't sure.

CHAPTER SIX

I JERKED my eyes open with a start.

At once, everything hit me.

I was at home. On my couch. With Chase.

A strange jangle sounded at the front of the house.

I sat up just in time to see the door fly open.

Drew bolted inside, keys in his hand and a look of panic on his face. Yes, I'd given him an extra key, just in case someone ever needed to get in. He apparently thought this was one of those occasions.

His concern quickly turned into a scowl when he spotted me . . . and then Chase.

Chase sat up behind me, staring back at Drew with disdain in his gaze.

Drew rushed toward me, ignoring Chase. "Holly . . . what happened? Are you okay?"

"I'm . . . I'm okay now. Why are you here?" I stood

and ran a hand through my hair, feeling entirely self-conscious.

"I got your text."

"What text?" What was he talking about?

He stared at me as if concerned I might be losing my mind. "The one you sent me yesterday evening saying you needed me. I drove all night to get here."

I shook my head. "I didn't send you a text, though."

He pulled out his phone and showed me the screen. "You clearly did."

I took his phone from him and stared at the words there. Sure enough, that was my number. My name.

But I hadn't sent that message.

The fact that my kidnapper had taken my phone and used it as part of his game caused another surge of anger to ignite inside me.

"I don't know what to say," I finally murmured, crossing my arms over my chest. "I didn't send that, Drew. I'm sorry this pulled you away from your conference. I really have no idea what's going on."

His gaze went to Chase, and he scowled again. "Is this what you do? You wait until Holly is at her most vulnerable and then you make a move?"

Chase rose, all six-plus feet of him. As he glanced at Drew, his muscles bristled. "You should watch yourself."

I stepped between them. I didn't fear a fist fight, but I didn't like the tension I felt.

"Drew, it wasn't like that," I said.

"Then what was it like? Because I walk in here and see you two sleeping together on the couch. What am I supposed to think?"

I knew how this looked. Not good. It was all my fault, and no one else's.

"I had a hard night, and I was scared," I started.

"So you found yourself in Chase's arms?" He stared at me, accusation in his eyes.

"Nothing happened." I didn't have to explain myself to Drew, yet I couldn't resist the urge.

"I guess you've made your choice then." Drew shook his head and stepped back. "I'm glad you're okay, but I expected more of you, Holly."

"Drew . . ." Defeat pressed on me.

Before I could say anything else, he stormed out the door, slamming it behind him.

I took a step after him, words failing me.

"Let him go, Holly," Chase said.

I buried my face in my hands, feeling like everything was crumbling around me. "I'm sorry, Chase. This is all my fault."

"It's okay, Holly. It's like you said, nothing happened."

"But it looks like it did. I think I was having a panic attack last night, Chase. I've never felt like that before. And I just couldn't be alone anymore—"

He grabbed my arm. "You don't have to explain yourself to me."

I glanced at him, my heart nearly melting at the protective look in his eyes. He knew my character. He knew my boundaries. We hadn't crossed that line. He respected me enough not to let that happen.

I let out a breath, trying to erase my guilt.

Everything just felt so tense and off balance right now.

"Listen, why don't you go get showered and dressed? Are you hungry?"

"I could eat something. Maybe toast."

"I'll make coffee and toast. And then we'll talk some more."

I nodded. "That sounds like a plan."

But I knew I still had a long road ahead of me before anything would feel okay. I only had five days until Sarah came home—that meant I had five days to get myself together.

I hoped I could do it.

———

AN HOUR LATER, I emerged from the bathroom. I'd taken an extra-long, extra-hot shower. I only wished the water would wash away the bad memories. But life wasn't that easy.

I hadn't even fixed my hair. I decided to let it air dry

today. It would end up wavy instead of with the smooth curls I liked. But I didn't care.

I padded down the hallway, in some ways dreading what today would hold. More memories and recollections. I also hoped it would provide more answers. The thought of that caused a surge of hope in me.

I paused in the kitchen doorway, feeling more self-conscious than I should. Chase sat at my kitchen table, the one I'd found at a thrift store and painted white. Early morning sunlight streamed inside through the windows behind the table. The soothing aroma of coffee floated through the air, the familiar scent washing over me and providing temporary comfort.

Chase . . . he looked so handsome as he sat there in a new T-shirt and jeans. His face looked fresh and clean-shaven. The brawny man showed his intelligent side as he studied the newspaper on the table. And last night . . . . he'd muttered that he loved me.

Certainly he hadn't meant it. It was the mixture of stress and high emotions. I needed to put that memory to rest and pretend like he hadn't said anything.

I swallowed the lump in my throat.

I'd never allowed myself to ever be as vulnerable with someone as I had last night with Chase. It wasn't like me, and I blushed at the thought.

Having him stay here had probably been a bad idea. I felt like I should regret it more. But I didn't.

Chase being here was the only reason I felt halfway alive this morning.

"Hey." He looked me up and down. "Jeans? In all the years I've known you, I hardly ever remember jeans."

I pushed a hair behind my ear self-consciously. He'd noticed.

After I'd showered, I'd stared at the dresses in my closet, the ones I normally loved to wear. But I couldn't bring myself to put one on today. Just the thought of donning a 50s-style outfit caused me to shudder, brought back too many uncomfortable memories.

"What can I say?" I shrugged, trying to make it seem like it wasn't a big deal. "I wanted a different look this morning."

"Both looks are nice."

My gut twisted. Since my abduction, I'd been thinking a lot about the way I'd idealized older time periods. Now, the thought of living in the 50s made me sick to my stomach.

That man had taken something away from me. Maybe not physically, but on a mental level. He'd taken my fascination with times past, and now I associated those golden decades with horrible memories.

I pulled my sweater closer around me and lowered myself at the table. Chase pushed some toast toward me. "It might be cold now. I didn't think your shower would be so long. Maybe I can warm it up?"

"No, it's fine." I was certain that whatever I ate would be tasteless and feel like a brick in my stomach.

"I'll get some coffee for you."

Chase rose, poured a cup, and set it in front of me. I took a sip, but the liquid made acid rise inside me. Nothing would taste good for a while. I felt certain of that.

"You probably need to go to work today," I finally said, absently rubbing my fingers on the side of the ceramic mug.

"I took the day off."

"I hate for you to waste your days off on me."

"You're never a waste, Holly." His voice sounded sincere, as did his eyes.

My cheeks flushed. For a moment, I remembered what he'd muttered last night. That he loved me. Had he meant the words? Or had they just been said in his sleepy state?

I'd been trying so hard to get this man out of my system. But the task seemed futile.

Our relationship had a tumultuous history. We'd been engaged. Then we'd taken a step back. Then I'd broken up with Chase—but only because I saw the writing on the wall.

Chase wasn't able to commit, and he wouldn't be able to until he dealt with some demons from his past. His half-brother had been murdered six years ago, and parts of the case were unresolved. Until Chase had some closure, I had my doubts that he'd ever be able to move on.

And I was ready for the rest of my life. All I'd ever wanted was to be a wife and mom. To keep a welcoming home. To be involved in the community.

Maybe it was one of the reasons I'd become obsessed with times past, with the 50s. I wanted that simplicity instead of the insane busyness of the world around me.

But I could feel that starting to change inside me.

Now I needed to figure out how to handle things with Drew as well.

However, my first priority right now was figuring out who had done this to me. I couldn't go on until I knew.

"Chase, this man has my phone, and he's continuing to send texts and making them seem like they're from me."

He pressed his lips together. "I know. Your purse was still here in the house. I don't think this guy was aiming to steal things from you. I think he wanted you, to mess with your head, your life."

I shuddered again. It just didn't make sense.

I cleared my throat, determined not to spiral into self-pity or fear. Not right now. "Any leads on who might be behind this?"

"I talked to Wilson this morning. The police still don't know much. They're going to check with the developer, Kurt Casey. Does that name sound familiar?"

I shook my head. "Not at all."

"The home you were in was a model home. That's why it was decorated."

My heart sank. That explanation seemed too easy. "Did other people have access to it?"

"I'm sure they did. Kurt Casey may have developed it, but he has a whole team of people who work for him. It will take a while to dig through everyone."

I let out a sigh and leaned back, picking at the crust of my toast. "I was thinking for almost the entire time I was in the shower about who might be behind this."

"Did you draw any conclusions?"

"I didn't. But I did feel like someone had been watching me over the past week or so."

Chase straightened. "What? Why didn't you tell me?"

I shrugged. "I thought I was being paranoid. I mean, I would turn around and no one was there. I had no evidence. No proof. No reason, even."

"Like I said, not everyone needs a reason."

"Honestly, I figured it was nothing."

Chase leaned toward me. "Did you think of anyone who's shown unusual interest in you lately? Now that you've had time to ponder it."

I frowned, hating to throw out a name, knowing the repercussions of an accusation like this. But I had to put my heart aside in the name of justice. "I'm not saying there's anything to this, but there was one man who came into my brother's office last week."

"What about him?"

"He was there to file a complaint about a new business slated to open near his neighborhood. It was a bar, and he didn't want the riffraff that would bring—his words, not mine. Anyway, before he left, he asked me out."

Chase raised his eyebrow. "What did you say?"

"I said no, of course. But he kind of looked at me strangely for a minute, and then he told me he didn't give up easily." I shifted as I remembered the way he'd said the words. The man had seemed so cocky and sure of himself. He'd rubbed me the wrong way.

"Do you have his name?"

"No, but it should be on file at the office."

"I'll need that."

"I'll get it for you."

Chase's phone dinged, and he looked at the screen. His eyes narrowed. "What . . . ?"

I wanted to look over his shoulder and see what the reaction was for. But I waited, minding my manners.

He shook his head and finally showed me the screen. The expression on his face clearly revealed that whatever it was disturbed him.

I had to stare at the video for several minutes before I realized what I was looking at.

It was me.

In bed last night.
Tossing and turning.
Someone had recorded it.
Ice climbed up my spine.
This wasn't over yet, was it?
No, it was far from over.

CHAPTER SEVEN

DETECTIVE WILSON CAME by and took my laptop. It appeared someone had managed to activate the webcam last night—I'd left my laptop open on my dresser—and had recorded me sleeping. Wilson also had his crew dust my place for fingerprints, and he swept the house for any other cameras.

He'd found none.

As I sat with my legs pulled beneath me on my couch, reality began to hit me. Reality of just how far this person was willing to go.

I wanted to believe the danger had ended when I was rescued, but I knew that was far from the truth. I pulled my favorite quilt up around my shoulders, suddenly chilled.

Ralph had gotten the name of the man who'd asked me out last week—it was Perry Gutherson. Another detective had already looked into him and discovered the man had been gone all week. None of his neighbors had seen him, but one did hear he was visiting his sick mother on the West Coast. That would need to be confirmed, of course.

But otherwise, it left me back at square one.

It wasn't the place where I wanted to be.

My doorbell rang. Chase walked in from the kitchen, where he'd been working at the table while I "rested" on the couch. His hand was at his waist, ready to draw the gun there if necessary.

He opened the door, revealing my best friend, Jamie. She stood there with her glowing brown skin, her springy black hair, and an urban sassiness that was unrivaled by anyone I'd ever met.

She ignored Chase and dashed toward me. "I know I wasn't supposed to come until after you rested, but I couldn't wait another moment. Are you okay? You've been all I could think about all night."

I sat up. "I'm okay. Thank you."

Jamie glanced back at Chase, a confused look on her face.

"Listen, I'll give you two a minute." Chase pointed behind him. "I'm going to make some phone calls."

As Chase disappeared into the other room, Jaime plopped beside me on the couch.

"What happened, girl?" She studied my face, her lips pulling down at the corners. "Everything has seemed classified or something. I've been out of my mind with worry."

I told her what had happened. Most of it, at least. I left out the part about Drew barging into the house this morning while Chase and I lay on the couch.

My cheeks still heated at the thought of it.

Her hand flew over her mouth as I talked. "That's so awful. Are you okay?"

I nodded, but the action took entirely too much effort. "Yeah, I'm fine. I mean, I'm as fine as I can be, you know?"

"Yeah, I know." She glanced over her shoulder before lowering her voice. "And Chase? I thought he was out of your life."

I shrugged. "He was supposed to drop off something for me that night. He got worried when I wasn't here. He hasn't left my side since he found me."

She let out a grunt. "That doesn't surprise me."

"Really?"

"Really. I don't know what's going on between you two, but it's special. You both just need to realize it. Chase needs to get over himself."

"Or maybe I just need to face the fact that we aren't meant to be." How much had to happen before I accepted that sometimes things just weren't meant to be? Our relationship had been through more twists and turns than a rollercoaster.

"Relationships are about two broken people real-izing that together they can be whole," Jamie continued.

I gave her a skeptical look.

She shrugged, looking unfazed. "Yes, I've been reading some relationship books. I figured it's good to stay on top of these things."

"Are you and Wesley having problems?" My friend had been head-over-heels happy since she'd started dating him. I hoped there wasn't trouble in paradise.

"No, not at all. But I like soaking in all the wisdom I can."

My smile turned into a frown. "As far as Chase and me . . . all I can say is that I've got bigger worries at the moment. I don't need any man drama to add to my list."

Jamie pulled her leg beneath her, a sympathetic look on her face as my words seemed to sober her. "I know you don't. Any idea who did this to you?"

"No idea whatsoever." If only I did. That would make my life so much easier right now.

She stared off in the distance, as if searching her thoughts before looking back at me and snapping her fingers. "What about that crazy girl who pretended to be your cousin?"

"What? You mean, Kari?" Kari Harling . . . I'd tried to put the woman out of my mind. She'd first shown up in my life, claiming to be someone named Blake and saying that we were related.

My father had been adopted, and we didn't know

anything about his biological family. Kari had said she was from his birth family. The problem was, we didn't even know who those people supposedly related to my father were, and every lead we discovered had only been a wild goose chase.

But I'd fallen for her story hook, line, and sinker. I'd even let her into my home when she was having financial problems. But, in the end, it had all been a lie. Blake hadn't been her real name. She wasn't a student at the University of Cincinnati. In fact, she'd been involved with some pretty shady people.

The biggest kicker had come the last time I'd seen her. Chase had revealed that, through some testing at the police department, my DNA and Kari's had shown we were, in fact, in some way related.

Then she'd disappeared, and I hadn't seen her since. I knew she was trouble, but I couldn't figure out what she was up to.

"We never found out what she was really planning," Jamie continued. "Maybe she was scheming all of this all along."

Though Kari still remained a suspicious character in my mind . . . "It was clearly a man who held me captive."

Jamie shrugged. "Maybe she was working with someone."

"I don't know . . . in my gut, it doesn't fit."

Jamie leaned closer, excitement building in her voice.

"Just think about it. It was weird how she appeared in your life and then disappeared. Whatever she wanted from you, she didn't get it. We don't even know what it was that she wanted. Maybe she hasn't given up."

"I suppose anything is worth looking into at this point."

She pursed her lips, her reporter instincts seeming to kick in. "You said no one owned that house where you were held captive?"

"That's my understanding. I'm hoping for an update later today. We'll see."

"These things take time, I know. But there's got to be a clue in there somewhere. Someone doesn't take that much time to set up something like this without leaving some kind of trail."

"That's what I'm hoping. I'm trying to let the police do their job. Normally, I'd try to be in the thick of things, but this is one instance where I'm probably better off staying on the sidelines."

"We'll see how long that lasts." Jamie studied my face. "Why do these things always happen to you?"

"That's a great question."

"I actually already know the answer. It's because you care. Because you go the extra mile. And, as a result, sometimes you stick your nose places where people don't want it."

"You'd think I would have learned my lesson by now . . ." Having a big heart seemed like a liability sometimes. I didn't want to acknowledge it, but, at some point, I'd need to face the truth.

"Don't change. The world needs more people like you, Holly Anna Paladin." Her gaze traveled down. "Speaking of which, what are you wearing?"

I shrugged at my jeans and T-shirt. "Somehow the 50s has lost its appeal."

"Don't let this psycho change you."

How could I go through something like that and not be changed? That was the bigger question that echoed in my mind. And the other question was, how was I ever going to continue on with life until this guy was caught?

I had no idea.

———

AFTER JAMIE LEFT AN HOUR LATER, all I could think about was how I wanted to be out on the streets myself. I wanted to track down answers. Figure out what had happened.

Jamie was right when she'd wondered how long my sideline position would last. I wasn't a sideline kind of girl.

Usually.

But right now I was trapped in my own home feeling clueless. The fact that I was clueless made me feel helpless, and my helplessness made me feel useless.

But what could I do other than contend with my

thoughts and let the police do their job? Chase was here, keeping an eye on me. My laptop was gone. I had no phone.

Quite honestly, part of me didn't want to leave the comfort of my home. I didn't want to face the world out there yet.

And that wasn't like me.

My doorbell chimed. My brother had called earlier and said he would stop by. He mentioned something about wanting to see with his own eyes that I was okay.

I peered out the window to confirm it was Ralph before opening the door. He'd brought his girlfriend, Olivia, with him.

Ralph and Olivia had only started dating three weeks ago, but she seemed to be becoming a fixture in his life. The two had nearly been inseparable since they met. I was really happy for him. Ralph's first wife had died in an auto accident shortly after they got married, and he'd been single for a long time.

"Holly, we were so worried." Olivia gave me a quick hug.

The woman was pretty—tall and slender, with dark hair she wore pulled into a bun. She owned her own grant-writing business and apparently did quite well with it. She always wore name-brand clothes, and she drove an expensive car. She fit right into my family of overachievers.

When she and Ralph had first started dating, I'd

done my own little online investigation into her. She'd passed my tests with flying colors. The woman was involved with charities, had won awards for her business, and liked to travel.

There was nothing not to like about her.

"No need to worry," I said. "I'm here. I'm fine."

As soon as Olivia stepped back, Ralph pulled me into an embrace. My brother was a nerdy cute guy who had an affinity for sweater vests—and it was sweater vest season again. How lucky for him.

I held back a smile.

"Can you really be fine after something like that?" Ralph murmured in my ear before stepping back. "You don't have to pretend with us."

My chin trembled and gave away my false bravado. "How about this? I *will* be fine."

Ralph gave me a brotherly glance and looked like he was about to say something when someone stepped up behind me.

"Chase." Ralph's voice held surprise.

My family knew all about my Chase drama. They liked Chase, but they were also protective of me, and I appreciated that fact. Like any good big brother, Ralph didn't want to see me get hurt.

"Ralph," Chase said. "Olivia."

Chase had met Olivia once at a community event. My family's presence and work in the area was practically legendary. Ralph, the state senator. My sister, Alex, a district attorney. Her husband was a doctor. My mom was a real estate agent and headed up so many committees that everyone knew her. She'd just married a retired cop.

"Are you investigating this case?" Ralph asked.

"No, I'm just here to support Holly."

Ralph gave me another look. I was sure he wondered what was going on with my life. My family had liked Drew. Of course, they'd liked Chase also. They just wanted what was best for me.

Unfortunately, everyone in my family thought they knew what was best for me instead of trusting me to make my own choices. It came with being the little sister.

"I can trade off with you," Ralph finally said. "If you need to take a break . . ."

I loved my brother. He was funny. Brilliant. Compassionate.

But he wasn't Chase.

"I'd feel better if I kept my eyes on her." Chase edged closer to me. "At least until we know more details about what's going on."

Ralph looked like he wanted to argue, but I saw Olivia squeeze his arm, and he backed down. "Whatever Holly wants."

"Whatever Holly wants," Chase repeated.

I shifted, feeling uncomfortable. Instead of

addressing the awkwardness, I cleared my throat and changed the subject. "I wonder how mom is doing."

Ralph turned toward Olivia and rested his arm around her waist. Olivia beamed up at him. "She's supposed to come home next week. She should be enjoying herself."

Though I didn't want to keep things from my mom, I was grateful she didn't know about this. I didn't want her to worry. Besides, she deserved some time to have fun. Her coming home early to dote over me wouldn't solve any problems.

As a moment of silence fell, Chase ran a hand across his neck and then over his face. "By the way, since you're here, how's your friend doing? The one you talked to me about."

I squeezed my eyebrows together. I had no idea what they were referring to. Had Chase and Ralph been chatting?

"He decided not to pay the money." Ralph frowned and then glanced over at me. "One of my old college buddies received a note with some questionable photos attached. Whoever sent it asked for money and warned not to get the police involved. He came to me for advice, and I talked to Chase about it—off the record."

"That's horrible that someone would blackmail him like that," I said. "Is he innocent or were the photos legit?"

"I'm not sure," Ralph said. "But either way, what's being done to him is wrong."

I froze as I heard a strange sound behind me. As I turned, I saw the TV flash on.

What?

I glanced at Chase, who looked equally as confused. No one in this room was near the TV or the remote.

A moment later, a man's face flashed on the screen . . . a man wearing a creepy mask.

CHAPTER EIGHT

"HELLO, HOLLY," the man crooned.

My knees went weak as everything around me began to spin. Chase caught me under my elbows and lowered me into a chair.

But my eyes were fastened to the TV screen. I couldn't look away, even if I wanted to.

The man sat in a room. On a stool. He wore black pants and a white shirt, along with the doll face mask. Behind him was a gray cement wall that looked dingy and old. The hair on his arms was dark. His skin was white, but not too pale. It had some tan to it. I couldn't see any other features.

"You took me by surprise—this time. But no more." The man sounded as even and controlled as he had before. "Next time, I'll take you by surprise. You're going to wish you'd never gotten away."

Then the TV went black, and the man was gone.

I reminded myself to breathe. But fear was a greater force. Everything inside and outside of me felt scrambled. Like there were moving parts. Too many. All around me. Like nothing made sense. Even though the room was still, all I felt was chaos.

"Holly?" Chase's face came into focus as he peered at me.

"How . . . ? I don't understand . . ." How had this man commandeered my TV?

"I need to call Wilson."

I nodded. As Chase stepped away, Ralph knelt beside me and Olivia stood behind him, a concerned expression on her face.

"That was the man who abducted you?" Ralph's voice sounded steely.

I nodded, wishing I could forget his image. His voice. The feel of his hands on my waist.

"Holly, why would someone do this to you?" Ralph continued.

I shrugged.

"You have no idea who that man is?" Olivia's eyes showed the terror I felt.

"No idea." I had no guesses. No leads. No anything.

"Oh, Holly . . ." Olivia squeezed my shoulder. "I'm so sorry. This is . . . terrifying."

Terrifying didn't begin to describe it.

Chase paced back over, sliding his phone into his pocket. "Wilson is coming over. We've got to figure out how someone managed to do that to your TV. Maybe we can trace the signal somehow."

I tried to nod, but I wasn't sure I actually did so. I kept replaying the image in my mind.

If only I'd pulled his mask off when I had the chance . . . maybe we could find this guy now. Maybe this nightmare could end.

Chase squeezed my shoulder. I knew he wanted to do something to make this better.

But the truth was that there was nothing anyone could do. This was my nightmare . . . and I was determined to live through it.

———

THREE HOURS LATER, the police left—with my TV and router and anything else electronic they could find. They'd muttered things to each other as they worked. Things about high-tech crimes, cyber criminals, extra precautions that might need to be taken.

I'd also heard them mutter the name the "Doll Man." Was that what they were calling this guy now?

I didn't ask.

I heard everything. Yet I didn't.

I preferred to sit on the couch staring stoically.

The whole day seemed to pass in slow motion. Right now, Chase was outside speaking privately with Wilson. As he did, something snapped in me.

I couldn't just sit here all day and feel sorry for myself. I wanted to do something.

I might not have a computer or a phone, but that didn't mean I couldn't sort out my thoughts. I pulled a notebook and pen from the drawer of my end table and sat back. I began jotting down everything I knew.

I knew this man was tech savvy. That he'd seemed to enjoy the process of scaring me. He knew I liked all things retro. He'd even found a retro-style house. He appeared to have no motive other than abducting me and forcing me to live a life I claimed I wanted. He enjoyed using my phone to raise the stakes.

Then I jotted the questions I had. The many, many questions.

How long had Doll Man been watching me?

What was his motive? I had a hard time believing it was ending his loneliness or fulfilling a fantasy. My logical side thought it seemed too farfetched. I wanted—needed—something more concrete.

Had he planned on keeping me at that house forever? It seemed unlikely since it was a model home.

Did that mean he had planned on killing me?

I shuddered.

Was the retro style a way of torturing me, of messing with my head?

I had so, so many questions.

The door opened, and Chase stepped back inside. "You want to get something to eat?"

"I'm not really hungry." Nor did I want to leave the house.

"Is there someone I can take you to?" He gently lowered himself onto the couch beside me. "Someone you could talk with?"

"I'm a huge proponent of counseling, but I'm not ready to go yet. I'm still processing."

He nodded, as if unsure what else to say. "I'm sorry this is all happening to you, Holly."

"Thanks, Chase. For everything you've done. I hate that you have to put your life on hold for all of this." I did. I wanted to make life easier for others, not become a burden to them.

"I would put my life on hold for you anytime."

The way Chase said the words made tingles go up my spine. I didn't dare look at him. I was afraid of what I'd see in his eyes. Afraid of what he might see in my gaze.

Finally, he cleared his throat. "I'd feel better if I stayed here again tonight."

Relief swept through me. "I'd feel better also."

"Maybe you should see if Jamie wants to stay too?" He rubbed his throat, as if emotions had lodged there. "Not that we need a babysitter, but . . . we should be careful, and I'd feel better if you had another set of eyes here."

I knew what he was doing, and I appreciated it. He was setting up boundaries and putting safeguards in place.

Last night had been innocent. But with emotions running as high as they were, we both needed to be careful right now. The next time might not be as innocent.

"I'll call her and see what she says."

Before I could reach for a phone, Chase's cell rang. I listened carefully as he answered and spoke to someone on the other line. When he ended the call, he turned back toward me.

"That was about the developer of the neighborhood where you were held," he said. "Kurt Casey."

"What about him?"

"The police are trying to track him down. But here's the interesting thing. The *Cincinnati Pilot* did an article on him about a month ago."

"What kind of article?"

"It was about how he liked all things vintage and retro. How he'd created this neighborhood for that very reason. The article even included pictures of the model home."

"That is interesting."

"Maybe you fit into his ideal for what life should be like."

I shrugged. It was a possibility. But could it really be that easy?

Not in my experience.

In the meantime, I just had to wait until the police found this guy and got some answers.

CHAPTER NINE

I WENT to bed early that evening. Jamie had come to stay with me, and it had been good to have her there to distract me with stories about her life. It had been good to have her close so I wasn't tempted to run into Chase's arms again.

But Jamie had left early this morning—5:30—so she could make it to an interview she was doing for the newspaper, one that required her to travel down to Kentucky. She'd been gone when I got out of bed.

I'd taken my time getting ready before pacing down the hallway. I had to brace myself for another day. I couldn't stand the idea of just staying inside for hour after hour with only my thoughts. Yet I also couldn't face the possibility of leaving my house again.

There was, however, one thing I had to do today. With Chase's approval, I'd jumped on his computer last night and sent a message under my own account. And now, in one hour, I would need to do something I dreaded.

Until then I would attempt to compose myself and eat some breakfast.

I paused in the kitchen. Just like yesterday morning, Chase sat at the table. He sipped on coffee and reviewed a file folder in front of him.

"You're awake," Chase started. "I've been waiting to talk to you."

"You have updates?"

He lowered the folder in his hands. "I do. Your tox screen came back. You were given a mix of drugs. Chloroform. Zolpidem. Xanax. It would be enough to knock you out for quite a while. They're also drugs that anyone could easily get—anyone with the right connections, at least. None of them are unique in the criminal culture, in other words."

"Okay . . ." I suppose that news didn't help us narrow down anything.

"Also, Wilson wants to keep your phone active, just in case this guy tries to use it again. Maybe we can ping the number and track him down. How do you feel about that?"

"Whatever it takes to catch him."

"That's what I thought you'd say. Next update." Chase drew in a long breath, looking like this one might be a real zinger. "The police were able to track down Kurt Casey."

I froze. "And?"

"He was . . . dead. It appears he put a gun to his head. Based on the financial problems he was having with his company, no one seems surprised."

I clenched my eyes shut. "I'm sorry to hear that."

"We all were."

"Will the police investigate to confirm that? Or was there a suicide note?"

"There was no note, and I'm sure they'll continue looking into it, especially considering the man's connection to your abduction."

Last night, I'd also borrowed Jamie's laptop. I'd done my own research into Kurt Casey, trying to see if anything about the man rang any bells. He didn't look familiar in the least. I'd even watched a video of him speaking at a luncheon, wondering if I'd recognize his voice.

I hadn't.

"Did you talk to anyone in the neighborhood where I was held captive? Did they see anything? Any strange cars?" I asked, still hoping for a breakthrough lead. To occupy my hands, I grabbed an orange from the bowl at the center of the table and began to slowly peel it.

Chase frowned. "No, no one saw anything. Because no one had heard from Kurt, several of the contractors assumed he'd skipped town over the financial troubles he was having with the company."

"What timing . . ." I knew that probably wasn't a coincidence.

"Exactly. Since residents can't move in yet, there was hardly anyone else around. We also checked security footage from traffic cams in the area. We haven't found anything yet."

It seemed impossible that there were no leads yet. I slowed down, drawing out the process of peeling the orange. "What about the way the man commandeered my TV yesterday? Did that give us any clues?"

"If so, we haven't discovered them yet. But I know Wilson and his team are still working on it."

I nodded. "I appreciate it. I really do. I just . . . I hate living like this."

Chase's gaze caught mine. "It's good to hear you say something other than that you're okay."

I said nothing for a minute.

"It's okay not to be okay," Chase continued, leaning toward me and touching my arm.

My throat burned. I knew his words were true, but . . . "I would just rather focus on other people instead of the attention being on me."

"That's a good way to live life—by putting others before yourself. It's what the Bible teaches. But there's nothing wrong with showing people who you really are either."

"You don't think I do that?" His words took my breath away. I'd always considered myself to be authentic. I pulled an orange slice from the sphere but couldn't bring myself to taste it.

"I think you always put your best foot forward. I just don't think it's healthy to stuff your feelings down inside."

I wanted to argue. I really did. But the words lodged in my throat.

Before I could respond, the doorbell rang. I knew who it was.

Drew.

I'd asked him to come.

And now we needed to have a talk. I put my orange down, promising myself I'd eat it later. And then I braced myself for the conversation ahead.

CHASE WENT BACK to the spare bedroom to work, giving Drew and I privacy in the living room.

Drew looked as dapper as always as he stood just inside the doorway with his black slacks, pinstripe shirt, and wavy dark hair. The man was the consummate gentleman. He believed in chivalry. He had impeccable manners.

He was basically a male version of myself. On paper, we should be perfect together. So perfect. We both even drove classic Mustangs.

"Holly . . ." Drew looked me over. "You don't look like yourself."

I'd worn jeans again today and a black T-shirt. My hair was naturally wavy, and I hadn't even put on any makeup.

"I thought I'd go for a more laid-back look for a change."

"You look nice." He smiled, but it looked forced.

"Can I get you anything?" I didn't even know what I had, but the words just came from me as naturally as some people breathed.

"I'm fine."

I nodded nervously and pointed behind me. "Maybe we should sit."

As I started to step back, he grabbed my arm. "Before we do, Holly—I'm sorry about the way I reacted to you yesterday morning." He frowned as he paused. "I was just so worried. And then I saw you. With Chase. My mind went to the worst-case scenarios. I know you said you needed some time . . . I should have kept myself in check."

I rubbed my arms. "I'm sorry you had to walk in on that. Whoever abducted me also took my phone. He must have sent you that message. Maybe he wanted you to come over just then because he knew . . ." Was that possible? Had that man been watching me? Had he known?

Drew's gaze darkened. "So whoever this is, he's playing games?"

"You could say that."

Drew dropped onto the couch and shook his head. "It makes me sick to my stomach to think about. I wish . . . I wish I could take it all away from you. That I could somehow change things."

I grabbed his hand and squeezed. "I know, Drew."

"It's hard sometimes to comprehend why such horrible things happen in life. Things that make no sense."

"That's the age-old question," I said. "I know hard times make us stronger. But, sometimes, things are just senseless. There is no reason that will make us feel better. We just have to determine that it's part of our story. Good or bad."

"You're a wise woman, Holly Anna." A sad smile flashed on his face. Sad probably because he knew life had taught me that lesson, starting with my father's death.

"I don't feel very wise." I frowned. "I like to pretend to be strong, but I feel like curling into a ball right now and hiding from the world."

"No one would blame you."

"I've just got to believe that the future is going to be brighter," I said softly. "If I don't believe that, then what do I have to hold onto?"

He said nothing for a moment. He only sat there, questions in his eyes.

My heart lurched in my chest, and, for a second, I doubted myself. I was probably about to make the biggest mistake of my life. And I had nothing to fall back on. But, in my gut, I knew what I had to do.

I drew in a deep breath before quietly saying, "I can't do this anymore, Drew."

"Do what?" He stared at me, confusion in his gaze.

"Us." A small sob escaped as I said the words.

He lowered his head. I couldn't see the pain in his eyes, but I somehow knew it was there.

"Is it because of Chase?" His voice sounded low, as if he fought emotions.

"I don't know what the future holds for Chase and me. But you and I . . . we're . . . well. It's just that . . . I don't know. It's like making a cake, I suppose."

Drew tilted his head toward me, now looking totally baffled.

I couldn't blame him. "It's like this. Sometimes, you have two really great ingredients like key lime and caramel. Alone, they each taste fantastic. But if you try to put them together in a cake, it just doesn't work. The tastes clash with each other."

"So I'm key lime and you're caramel?" His lips twisted with confusion.

I shrugged. "Kind of. I mean, it's hard to say. It's just that we should be perfect together—"

"Then why aren't we?" His eyes probed mine.

That was a great question. But I'd come this far. I couldn't skate around the truth now. "For some reason, when I'm with you, Drew, I have this need to be perfect. This pressure. You don't put it on me. I put it on myself. But I can't shake it."

"You know I don't want you to feel that way." His voice held both passion and sincerity.

"I do. I know that. But, for some reason, I can't change it." I'd tried to come to terms with it. To deal with it. And I couldn't.

His face tensed, and he glanced at his hands for a moment before softly saying, "It was because of when I had you work at the funeral home, wasn't it?"

I remembered that awful day. The day I'd had to try to comfort mourner after mourner. People I didn't know. People who grieved great losses.

It had taken me back to so many hard places in my own life. Especially losing my father.

And I'd known that would be expected of me if I married Drew. It was a family business. A business where death was a way of life.

I'd hated every minute of it.

I slowly bobbed my head up and down. "That was eye-opening for me. I guess I want to be all prim and proper on the outside. But, on the inside, there's a bit of rebel there. Most people don't see it. But I only like the confines of etiquette when it doesn't smother me. When it's forced on me, when I need to break out of the box . . . I need the freedom to do so."

"But you're always prim."

I let out an airy laugh. "Some people would disagree. Like when I broke into that house to clean it . . ."

"True."

"Or when I disregard the rules in order to help someone. I seem like I stay within the lines, but I don't. That's really what it boils down to. I like doing things on my terms."

He glanced down and remained silent a few minutes. "I had a feeling this was coming."

"I'm sorry, Drew." I was. I hated hurting people. Hated it.

"I am too. But . . . at least we know now, right?"

"At least." My voice cracked.

He looked up and drew in a breath as if trying to pull himself together. "You've been a joy in my life, Holly. There will never be anyone else like you."

I smiled my first true smile in days. "I feel the same about you, Drew. Sincerely."

He stood, and I followed his lead. Stiffly, he pulled me toward him in a loose hug. "I wish you the best of luck. And I hope they find the person who did this to you."

"Thank you, Drew."

I watched as he left, my heart heavy.

But, as I turned around, Chase stood there.

I thought he might remark on what had just happened. Instead, he had a new look in his eyes.

"I think we have a lead," he said.

"Really?"

"I'm not sure if it fits in with this case or not, but I think it's something you're going to want to pursue."

"What's it about?"

His lips flickered with the start of a grin. "It's about Kari Harling."

I sucked in a breath. "What?"

He nodded. "You were talking about her yesterday, wondering if she could be linked to what happened. I'm not saying she is. But I am saying that I think I found her."

CHAPTER TEN

MY LUNGS FELT like cement had been poured into them as I waited to hear what Chase had found. I lowered myself back onto the couch.

I'd been trying to track down Kari myself for the last several months, but I'd had no luck. Then again, I didn't have the same resources the police department did either. My methods had included online searches and generally keeping my eyes open for her.

"I've had a trace on her for a while." Chase sat down across from me. "If her credit card was used, if her name came up in the system for any reason, or her driver's license—anything. But it's been radio silent. Nothing. It's like she disappeared off the face of the earth, just as you said."

"Okay . . ." My hands twisted together in my lap as I

waited for him to continue. I had to know where he was going with this.

"Last night, I decided to have several variations of her picture made by the forensic artist at the station. Some with her hair dark. Others with it short. There were probably six different images in the end. I was hoping to get a hit on at least one of them."

I sucked in a quick breath. "And I'm assuming you did get a hit?"

"While you were talking to Drew, I got a call from one of the beat cops who works in the Queensgate area. There is someone who looks like Kari who's been hanging out near a warehouse there."

My pulse spiked. "Okay then. That sounds like good news."

"She appeared to be homeless."

His words caused the breath to leave my lungs. "Homeless?"

In all my imaginings, I hadn't expected that. I'd expected Kari might be involved in drugs or conning people or involved in some kind of crime ring. Things that would make me dislike her—not feel sorry for her. I didn't *want* to feel sorry for her.

Chase caught my gaze. "I'm not saying she is homeless. Just that she appears to be."

"That's . . . terrible." I didn't know what else to say.

He raised his hand, as if to stop my thoughts before they veered me into Guiltville. He knew me too well.

"My guys are checking the warehouse right now, the one where she's been spotted."

"And?"

He shrugged. "And they'll let me know what they find out."

I stood. Queensgate wasn't terribly far from where I lived. It would only take us ten minutes to drive there. If the cops found Kari, I wanted to see her with my own eyes, to talk to her.

"Can we go?" I asked, my voice coming out small and nearly childlike.

"Go where?"

"To the warehouse."

He gave a quick shake of his head. "That doesn't seem like a great idea. Besides, I thought you wanted to stay put."

Excitement flared to life in me, making me feel more alive than I'd felt since the abduction. "I do, which is exactly why I need to get out."

Chase remained still. "What will it prove if you go down there?"

"I want to talk to her in person."

"She's probably not connected to this case. You know that, right?"

"Even more reason to talk to her. It will get my mind off things. Besides, the police are there checking things out. The area will be secure, right?"

"I suppose." He still looked hesitant.

"Please?" I finally asked.

Chase let out a long breath. "Okay. But if anything seems suspicious, you're staying in my car where it's safe. Do you understand?"

Hope spread through me as I nodded. "I understand. Thank you."

———

MY THOUGHTS still raced as I headed with Chase down the road in his police sedan. I much preferred the safety of my own home right now. But answers called to me. I needed to know the truth, if not about my abduction then about the con artist turned homeless woman known as Kari Harling.

"Do you think Kari has any part in what happened to me?" I asked, watching as the city blurred past my windows.

Chase let out a breath as he gripped the steering wheel. "I have no idea. But I think we should pursue it, considering everything that happened between the two of you. This woman was obsessed with you. Whoever is behind this is obsessed with you."

"But the person who abducted me is a man, a man who has means and who's tech savvy. I don't know about Kari being connected with this."

"I agree that it seems like a stretch. But I still think it's worth pursuing."

"I think so too."

We continued down the road, the area around us growing more rundown. More graffiti covered. More gang infested. We were in what some people called the hood.

The hood didn't scare me. I'd been a social worker for many years, and these places had been a part of my territory.

Though low economic status did sometimes go hand in hand with crime, that didn't mean I feared the people who lived with very little means. In fact, my heart went out to them.

Chase pulled to a stop in front of an old brick-fronted warehouse. The windows had wood covering them. Spray paint let people know this wasn't their territory. Even the sky seemed bleaker here.

The good news was that it was daytime, and I didn't see anyone wandering around the area looking to start trouble. Maybe that was because three police cars were parked nearby.

Still, Chase looked apprehensive as he put his car in Park.

"So this is where Kari was last seen?" I asked, trying to imagine her here. She seemed so much like the girl next door when I first met her. I couldn't even put the two pictures together in my mind.

"That's correct. She's been hanging out outside this building for at least a few weeks."

My stomach tightened at the thought. What if she *was* homeless? What was this woman's story? What was the truth?

I had no idea. But I desperately wanted to find out. I also reminded myself she was a con artist. This could all be a part of her plan.

An officer stepped out of the warehouse and glanced at Chase.

"Stay here," Chase ordered. "Until I find out what's going on. Promise?"

"Promise."

With one last glance at me, Chase climbed out. I watched as he met with the officer. They chatted several minutes before Chase came back to the car and opened the door.

"The area is clear," he said.

My stomach sank. "No Kari?"

"No, but there is some evidence that she could be living here."

"What's that mean?"

"It means I'm going to go check it out. Please don't make me regret asking you this, but do you want to come?"

I hesitated for only a moment before pushing Doll Man's face out of my mind. "Yes, I do."

"Then let's go. Remember—stay close."

Based on the fear coursing through me, I had no doubt I would be doing just that.

———

I HELD onto Chase's arm as we stepped into the abandoned warehouse.

A huge room stretched in front of us, and I suspected there used to be assembly line-like equipment here. Now, broken windows trimmed the top of the space, allowing in grayish-tinted light.

The whole place smelled musty and like urine.

Maybe I'd seen too many movies, but it just seemed like the kind of building where bad things happened.

I swallowed hard and held on to Chase's arm.

As we walked across the open space, I glanced down. This building was supposed to be abandoned, but there was evidence that people had been in here recently. Soda bottles. Beer cans. Chinese food containers. Snack wrappers.

Chase swept a flashlight beam across the floor as we walked, our footsteps echoing in the building. Though officers guarded the perimeter, this whole place just felt ominous.

We headed toward the back of the building. Apparently, there were offices there, some storage areas, and rooms on a second level that overlooked the production area.

Was Kari really hanging out here? The word on the street might be that she was living here now, but this didn't seem like a place anyone would want to live.

We stepped into the hallway. Chase swung the beam of his flashlight into the office. It illuminated a sleeping bag on the floor, along with a pillow.

"Someone has been living here," Chase said quietly.

It appeared to be a female—maybe. The bag was pink, at least. And there was a hairbrush beside the bed. Maybe the police could test the DNA samples there. Kari had several connections with some minor crimes in the area, which was the only reason Chase could utilize this manpower right now. The police had never been able to find her, nor had she been a top priority.

Maybe we were onto something.

But if Kari lived here, where was she now?

Had she run when she heard the police enter the building?

"We'll come back to this room in a moment," Chase said. "I want to check out the rest of the place first."

He continued down the quiet hallway, his light sweeping the floor.

As we stepped around the corner, a squeak sounded above us.

We froze.

Someone was in here.

The noise had been too loud to be a mouse or other small creature. No, it had sounded like a footstep.

Chase looked at me. "Wait right here."

My throat tightened. I didn't want to be left alone.

But I wasn't sure I wanted to go upstairs either. Especially since I wasn't sure whom I'd face.

I shook my head. The police had cleared the building. I should be safe.

Still, fear tiptoed across my skin. I pressed myself into a corner while Chase took the steps.

I knew he was trying to watch out for my safety, in case there was something dangerous upstairs. But I hated being alone. And I really hated being alone in the dark.

Dear Lord, help me now. Help us to find answers.

As I said "amen," someone whispered my name.

I shook my head. No, I'd been hearing things. I must have been. Who would say my name?

Except maybe Kari.

Was she here? Was she watching me right now?

"Holly . . ."

I heard it again. My name. A high-pitched voice whispered it so quietly, it sounded like feathers touching the ground.

I glanced back at the staircase Chase had climbed. I should wait for him.

But what if it was Kari? What if she was going to get away?

Slowly, with my back pressed against the wall, I headed down the hallway. Back toward the office.

What if she'd been inside? What if she'd been hiding when we checked out the space?

But as I turned the corner, I froze in my tracks.

Kari Harling wasn't standing there.

It was the man in the mask. The man who'd abducted me. Doll Man.

I tried to scream, but nothing left my throat.

The terror that had been tiptoeing across my skin now scrambled in a full-fledged panic.

My abductor was back.

CHAPTER ELEVEN

"I WAS HOPING I might find you here," he whispered, stepping closer.

His mask made me feel like I was talking to a psychopath. The expression painted there made him look so happy. So harmless.

I scooted back, but not nearly fast enough. Where was my voice? My reflexes?

Neither fight nor flight kicked in. Instead, I was frozen.

I couldn't break myself out of the moment.

Chase! I mentally screamed his name. But the word wouldn't leave my lips.

"You didn't think you'd get away that easily, did you?" He moved closer and closer. "I always finish what I start."

All I could hear was myself breathing. Breathing rapidly. Way too shallow.

I pressed myself into the wall as sweat scattered across my already clammy skin.

Images sliced into my mind. Images of me waking up in the strange house. Of the man touching my waist. Standing close. Acting like I was his wife and we lived in a different time period.

"You're going to need to come with me." Doll Man grabbed my wrist.

As I felt his touch, something sprang to life inside me.

"No!" The sound came out as a half yell, half scream.

I would not go with this man. Not if I could help it.

The man stiffened as footsteps sounded above me.

Then he ran.

Go after him!

But I couldn't. Instead, I collapsed on the floor, my entire body seeming to shut down.

The officers were out there. Certainly they would catch him. Stop him. Right?

Oh, Lord. Help me!

The Doll Man had been here. If he'd had a knife, he could have killed me.

"Holly?" Chase appeared from the stairway and sank down beside me.

I pointed in the distance. "He was here. He went that way."

Chase stared at me another moment, as if contemplating whether or not to leave.

He stayed.

"Chase?"

As he moved to the side, I saw someone behind him. Kari Harling.

I knew he didn't trust her and didn't want to leave me with her. Instead, he grabbed his radio and called the incident in. Then he helped me to my feet.

His entire body felt tense as his arm wrapped around my waist.

I glanced back at Kari, trying to get a good look at her. She was handcuffed. She'd been crying. And she looked dirty, with matted hair, dirty skin, and torn clothes.

Too many dilemmas hit me at once. The heartbreaking reality of seeing her like this. The reminder of what she'd done to me. Coming face-to-face with my abductor. The fact that they'd both been in the same place at the same time.

I couldn't wait to get out of this dingy warehouse.

Was anywhere safe? It sure didn't feel like it.

———

CHASE, Kari, and I emerged from a door at the side of the building. Chase had one arm around me and his other hand gripped Kari's arm.

The sunlight nearly blinded me, and I squinted, desperate for a glance of Doll Man. I needed to see him being captured. To know he hadn't gotten away again.

Instead, a chain-link fence stared back. Trash collected along its edge, as well as some dried leaves. But there was no sign that anyone had just come through here.

Chase led both of us to the front of the building, his steps taking on an urgent pace. Neither Kari nor I said anything. The conversation I needed to have with her would require time, not quick snippets, so I'd saved my breath—for now.

As we reached Chase's car, he turned to his officers. They all shrugged, as if nothing had happened.

"Did you find him?" Chase demanded.

"We didn't see anyone," one said.

"You didn't see anyone come out of the building?" Chase's voice grew louder with intensity.

"No, sir."

"If that's the case, he must still be inside. Go search for him. Now."

The three officers scrambled into action.

Chase led Kari to the back of his car and ushered her inside.

"I'll get back to you in a minute." He slammed her door shut and turned toward me, his gaze softening. "Did he hurt you?"

I shook my head, angry at the stray tear that rolled down my cheek. I quickly wiped it away. "No."

"What did he say?"

The moment flashed back to me. "That he always finishes what he starts."

Chase's face turned red. "He just came out of nowhere?"

"Maybe he came from the office." I wasn't sure. I hadn't thought things through yet. I'd only reacted.

Chase's jaw tensed. "I don't like where any of this is going."

"I don't either."

One of the officers approached, almost looking timid around Chase. "We didn't see anything, sir."

"This man didn't disappear," Chase growled. "He went somewhere. Keep searching."

"Yes, sir." The officer scrambled away.

Chase turned back to me. "Did you hear a door opening? Anything that would give an indication as to where he went?"

"No . . . I'm sorry. I just froze up. I could hardly do anything. Until he grabbed my wrist. And then panic set in."

"I should have never brought you here." He pulled me into a hug.

"At least you found Kari."

He stepped back, his gaze darkening. "The fact that

she was here as well as this guy . . . it makes me think they were working together."

I swallowed hard at the thought.

"As soon as we have some resolution on this man who was inside, I'll question Kari."

The minutes passed, and I could feel Chase's thoughts turning. He wasn't happy. The waiting was killing him.

But I knew he didn't want to leave me again, and I appreciated the sentiment. I didn't want to be left.

Finally, another officer appeared. This time, he held something in his hands.

It was a mask.

My knees went weak when I saw it. It was the man's. It was definitely the man's.

"He must have taken off his disguise and walked right out into the public," Chase muttered, opening an evidence bag he'd grabbed from his trunk. "We need to check the cameras in the area. Certainly someone saw something."

"I'll get right on that, sir."

But I had little hope they would discover anything. This guy was too good. Too smart and too determined.

CHAPTER TWELVE

I SAT in the employee lounge at the police station while Chase and Wilson interrogated Kari. I wanted to be in there. I wanted to hear what she was saying. But I knew there were professional boundaries that needed to be kept, and I tried to be respectful.

But I kept replaying what had happened in the warehouse. If Doll Man had wanted to, he could have killed me today. I'd been an easy target.

So why hadn't he? Did he want me alive for some reason? Had his goal been to abduct me again?

Nothing made sense.

My heart pounded. Someone had brought me some coffee, but the liquid turned my stomach. I left the cup on the magazine-littered table beside me. It didn't matter—the drink was now cold.

Finally, Chase stepped into the lounge and met my gaze. "Come with me."

I followed him into his office. He sat down in a chair in front of his desk, and I took the one beside him. My stomach churned even harder as I anticipated what he might tell me.

"I don't believe Kari Harling has anything to do with what happened to you this week," Chase started.

"But that man was there."

"I know. I know how it looks. But I believe that this man is somehow monitoring us. I believe he knew we were going there, and he was waiting for us."

"How would he do that?"

"That's what we're trying to figure out."

I rubbed the skin between my eyes, trying to ward off a headache. "What did Kari say?"

Chase stood and grabbed a bottle of water from a cabinet behind him. "She said she's basically homeless. She's been staying there for a few months. She said she's never seen that man before. She actually shuddered when she looked at the mask."

"She's a great actress," I reminded him.

"I know." He paced back over toward me.

I glanced at my hands. I'd picked all my pink nail polish off over the past couple days, and now my nails looked ragged and very unlike me. I supposed it fit my emotional state right now, though.

"I just don't understand all of this," I whispered.

Chase sat back down beside me, holding his water. He looked exhausted. Why hadn't I noticed that before? This was all wearing on him also.

"I don't either, Holly. But we're trying to find answers. I promise you that."

I raised my head. "Can I talk to her?"

He took a long sip of his drink before saying, "When Wilson is done with her. She's here willingly. We haven't charged her with anything."

"Okay." As the word left my lips, the door burst open. Jamie stood there, wide eyes full of panic.

Her shoulders slumped when she saw me.

"You're okay," she muttered, leaning against the door.

"Why wouldn't I be okay?"

"I got a text from you. It said that someone was trying to kill you and that I needed to get to the police station right away. That your life depended on it."

I exchanged a look with Chase.

It was the man again. He was playing more games.

When would this end? Or would it only be over when I was dead?

———

JAMIE LEFT AN HOUR LATER, after we'd convinced her that I was okay. Though she'd known my phone had been stolen, she feared I'd gotten a new one and sent that message. Either way, she wasn't taking any chances. Like any great friend, she'd been determined to check on me.

What a disaster.

Thankfully, I was cleared to talk to Kari about that same time. Since Kari wasn't officially a suspect, there was less red tape to cut through. The police let me into the interrogation room, and I sat across from her. No one else was in the room with us.

She looked like a shell of the person I'd first met. When she'd shown up at my door initially, she'd reminded me so much of me. Same haircut. Same lilt in her voice.

Right now, her hair was a darker brown than mine and appeared dull and tangled. Dark circles hung beneath her eyes.

Chase had said he'd come in with me, but I wanted to talk to her alone. I needed her to open up to me.

I wanted to know why she'd played me. Why we had markers in our DNA that proved we were somehow related. There was so much that didn't make sense.

"Long time no see," I started, lacing my fingers together on the table.

Kari averted her gaze to the floor. "I know."

I thought I was going to be tough and that all the righteous anger I felt toward her would be put to good use. Instead, I just felt sorry for the woman. Maybe I was too kind-hearted for my own good. I had been told that before.

"Who are you?" I asked. "Is Kari Harling even your real name?"

She shook her head. "It's Kari Leblanc, officially."

The new last name didn't ring any bells. "Why did you track me down and target me?"

She shrugged, her gaze still downcast. "It's a long story."

"I have time." I had nothing but time right now.

She let out a long breath and rubbed her cheek. She seemed to have aged a decade since I'd seen her. "I used to be kind of normal. Like you. Then my mom died, and my life was turned upside down, to say the least."

"I'm sorry."

"My grandma filled in since my dad was a no-good louse. Before she died, Grandma admitted that she'd had a son she gave up for adoption shortly after he was born. She said she was poor and didn't have much money. And she wasn't married, which at the time was especially taboo."

"Okay." I wasn't sure where Kari was going with this, but she had my attention.

"I'd given a baby up also, and I regret it every single day. It got me thinking about my grandmother's first-born son—my dad's brother. It became my life's mission to track him down. I wanted to know how he turned out. If he was okay. If my baby would be okay."

"And?" Kari's story was compelling and had sucked me in. But I needed to remain unemotional. I had to remind myself of that fact over and over again.

She shrugged. "And I found out that my uncle was Herbert Paladin."

I sucked in a breath. I'd suspected that was where this was going, but I wasn't ready to believe it. Her uncle was my father. I'd discovered my dad was adopted, but I didn't know any details about his birth family.

I couldn't take her word for it, though. "How did you track him down? It was a closed adoption."

Kari shrugged, like it was all in a day's work. "I'm from a small county in West Virginia. I was able to find the nurse who helped deliver the baby and secure the adoption. I kept connecting the dots until it led me to your family. However, I found out that my uncle had died. And then I got scared."

"Scared of what?" Now she wasn't making sense.

"Scared of how you all would react. Scared of what doors I might be opening up. So instead, I started to watch you. I became jealous. You had the life I'd always wanted." Her voice caught with a new emotion.

"Me?" I squeaked.

"Yes, you. You had the handsome boyfriend. Two of them, kind of. A close-knit family. A nice home. A good career."

"What was your family like?" I needed more information so I could paint a complete picture. I needed to put aside Holly Anna Paladin, the scorned woman, and tap into Holly Anna Paladin, the counselor.

"My dad liked to drink too much. He couldn't hold down a job. We were on welfare. It wasn't exactly a happy childhood." Each word was edged with bitterness.

"I'm sorry to hear that."

She looked up, her gaze filled with . . . envy? Admiration? Jealousy? "Then I saw you, and I . . . well, I wanted to be you. I got my hair cut. I got a job that didn't pay much, but it did allow me to buy some clothes. I even applied to go to UC and got accepted."

"And then you decided to introduce yourself to me . . ." My throat tightened as I was reminded of the betrayal.

"That's right. I worked up the courage. But I couldn't bring myself to tell you who I really was. I chickened out."

"I believe you—up until this point of the story. Kari, in case you don't remember, when we first met, you sent me on a wild goose chase. You told me my father's birth family was a group of people who were actually unrelated to my father. Plus, there are a million other things that don't make sense."

She pushed her hair behind her ears, her eyes welling with moisture. "I know. It's complicated, like I said. But when you're desperate for food and money, you'd be surprised the things you might do."

She wasn't getting off the hook that easily. "I tried to help you. I let you stay in my house."

"I know but—"

Before she could answer, someone banged on the window. The door opened, and Wilson stepped in. "I hate to cut this short, but we need to use this room. Ms. Leblanc, you're free to go. We're not charging you with anything—this time."

She stood quickly and nodded equally as fast. "Thank . . . thank you."

Disappointment swelled inside me. I'd hoped for more. But maybe we could continue this conversation later.

As I stepped with Kari into the hallway, I turned toward her, more questions filling my head. "Where will you go tonight?"

She shrugged. "Maybe back to the warehouse. It isn't as bad there as you might think."

"You can't go there." I didn't trust the woman, but I couldn't stand the thought of her living on the streets.

"Like I said, it isn't as bad as you think. It's warm. I have a little bed. It could be a lot worse."

I frowned. I couldn't ask her into my own home. Not after everything that had happened. But I knew I had to do something.

"Chase and I will drive you to a motel, and I'll pay

for you to stay there," I announced, my voice leaving no room for argument.

I wouldn't give her cash. I didn't trust her enough. But I would pay for her room myself.

"You don't have to do that." She shook her head and stepped back, her actions jerky and uncertain.

"I want to and, in return, I want to talk to you more. I need more answers."

Kari stared at me a moment as if contemplating her choices. Finally, she nodded. "Okay then. Thank you."

Maybe I would finally have some closure . . . to this mystery, at least.

CHAPTER THIRTEEN

CHASE and I dropped Kari off at a motel located about five miles from my house. It wasn't the nicest establishment in the area, but it wasn't the worst either. It had doors that opened to the outside, free breakfast, and was in a decent area of town.

Kari hadn't said much on the drive there. I didn't say much either. There would be time to talk later. In the morning, I would bring her some clean clothes so she could take off the dirty, ripped outfit she had on.

I couldn't be certain, but I thought I saw sincere gratefulness in her gaze as she'd told me thank you.

I knew Chase wasn't on board with any of this, but he'd supported me, saying very little throughout the whole process.

"Listen," he finally said once we were back in his car. "What do you think about staying at my place tonight?"

"Your place? Really?"

He shrugged. "I feel like your house has been compromised too many times. I'd feel better if you stayed with me."

"What about Jamie?" It was one thing to have her stay at my place. It was another thing to ask her to keep changing locations just so she could chaperone us. It seemed weird, and the thought of it made me uncomfortable.

"She's welcome to stay also."

"But if she can't . . . we're two adults, right? I mean, we'll be okay on our own. With boundaries."

"Absolutely."

I offered a quick clipped nod, determined to make this work. I mean, I could stay at Ralph's, but that was just weird. My mom wasn't home. My sister had a baby in the house. I could stay at Jamie's, but she had little brothers. I didn't want to put anyone in danger.

Chase made the most sense. I just had to come to terms with the history between us.

"Okay," I finally said. "That's fine. I just need to swing by my place and get some clothes."

He reached into his glove compartment. "And this is for you."

I took the object he handed me. It was a phone. "When did you get this?"

"I had one of my guys pick one up. Hopefully you'll get your laptop back soon, as well."

"I've always said I didn't love technology, so this has been a chance to get away from it all." I tried to sound amused, but the truth was, it had been challenging.

The other truth was that the idealistic version of myself was beginning to shrivel. I could feel it. And I didn't know what to do about it. To let it die? To try and keep it alive?

The good news was that I didn't have to decide right now.

———

I GLANCED around Chase's place as I stepped inside. His house looked just as I remembered. I hadn't been here in a good six months.

It was a total bachelor pad, and I would love to get my hands on the rooms and add a little warmth to them. But the simple decor fit Chase.

"What did you think about my conversation with Kari?" I asked, putting my bag on the floor. I'd wanted to wait until we had some uninterrupted time before I asked him that question.

I knew he'd been listening to everything on the other side of the glass.

He let out a long breath. "It's hard to say. It's like you mentioned earlier—the woman is a con artist. You have to take everything she says with a grain of salt."

"If what she said is true . . . I have family members living in West Virginia whom I never knew existed."

"It doesn't necessarily sound like they're people you're going to be clamoring to get to know."

I nodded in agreement. "How do I even go about proving any of this?"

"It will require searching records, talking to people, maybe even some DNA tests."

"Maybe after this guy is caught . . ." I shivered. "I still can't get past the fact that Kari and Doll Man were both in the same place at the same time."

"He could have followed her there. Followed *us* there, for that matter."

"How did he get past all those cops?"

"There are several entrances to the building, but my guys also discovered a basement with a walkway connecting that building to another in the next lot. Both warehouses used to be owned by the same company."

"And what about Kari? Where was she when your guys swept the place?"

"She'd hidden in a closet. She thought we'd left, and that's when she came out. However, you and I were just below her when she did, so we heard her."

I sighed. There was so much to comprehend.

I glanced at my watch. I needed to call Sarah.

My heart lurched as I thought about her. She was only fourteen, and she'd been my foster daughter for three months. She had Type 1 diabetes, and our time together had been challenging. But we'd bonded.

Though I was rooting for her to be permanently reunited with her birth mom, there was a part of me that didn't want her to either. But I knew that was selfish. I had to want what was best for her.

I loved the girl dearly. Though I was glad she wasn't here this week with everything that happened, I still missed her.

My gut told me our time together was quickly coming to an end. The fact that she'd been approved to spend a week with her mom only solidified the sentiment. I knew the reality of foster care, but, still, the thought of her leaving was so hard.

"Can you excuse me for a minute?" I asked Chase.

"Of course." He motioned for me to follow him down the hallway. He pushed a door open. "It's not much, but you can sleep here tonight."

"Thank you." I slipped past him, grateful for a safe place to stay, yet feeling all out of sorts. Maybe talking to Sarah would make me feel better.

I could only hope so.

CHAPTER FOURTEEN

AS SOON AS Chase closed the door, I dialed Sarah's number. She answered on the first ring. "Hello?"

"Sarah, it's Holly. I have a new number."

"Holly! I almost didn't answer. I'm glad I did. I've missed you." Her voice rose with sweet innocence.

My heart warmed as I lowered myself onto the bed. I'd missed that voice. "I've missed you too. How are things going?"

"I love Orlando, Holly," she said. "All the amusement parks are great."

Sarah's mom had won a trip through one of the recovery programs she'd graduated from. "I'm so glad to hear that. You only have four more days until you come back to me."

"I know. I can't wait. I mean, I'll miss Mom when I'm back, but . . . I don't know. It's confusing."

I swallowed the lump in my throat. "It is confusing. It's okay to miss us both in different ways and at different times. But I'm glad you're having fun now. Your diabetes has been okay?"

"It's been fine. I've remembered my insulin and to check my blood sugar."

"Good girl."

"Okay, we're going to go watch a parade tonight, so I've got to go. Thanks for calling!"

I smiled at the excitement in her voice. "Okay, watch that parade and get lost in the magic!"

"Oh, and Holly? Why did you send me a video of our house?"

I froze. "What are you talking about?"

"Yesterday I got a video from you in my email. It showed the front of our house. There were no words, just heavy breathing, like you were out of breath. It was kind of weird. I assumed it was so I wouldn't forget you."

My stomach clenched yet again. This guy was getting to Sarah now? That wasn't okay.

"That was weird, wasn't it?" I tried not to concern her too much. She was in Florida, far away from all of this. She should be safe. "But if you get any more messages supposedly from me, let me know. I'm afraid someone is trying to play some practical jokes on me."

"People are weird."

Doll Man's face flashed in my mind again. "Tell me about it."

"Okay, talk to you later. Love you, Holly!"

"I love you too!"

———

I MET Chase back in his living room. I sat beside him on the couch, my thoughts racing. I told him about the video, and he looked upset, as I knew he would be. This guy had been outside my house. He'd probably taken the video from his car.

And we'd been none the wiser.

"Have there been any pings on my phone? Any leads?" I asked. If not, I wanted to shut that number down before the man could do any more damage.

"Apparently, this guy has been able to redirect the pings, so it's been a bit of a wild goose chase. But they're still hoping for a breakthrough." Chase paused. "I did hear something else as well. My guys talked to some people who frequently hang out around the warehouse where we found Kari. Two of them said they saw Kari talking to a man with dark hair. They said he looked out of place in the area."

"Do they know who he is?"

"We're looking into it."

I nodded before launching into another idea I'd had. "I had a thought."

"What's that?"

"The mask that man wore—"

"We're testing it for DNA right now."

"I figured you were. And I hope they find something, but I was thinking—it may be a custom mask. I mean, I've never seen one like it before."

"Okay . . ."

I pulled my legs beneath me. "Well, how many companies make masks like that? I can't imagine there would be that many."

"You're probably right."

"I was hoping that maybe we could look online and see what we can find out."

"It can't hurt." Chase grabbed his laptop and set it on his lap. After the screen flashed on, he typed in "customized masks." Several pages of results came up.

"Maybe refine it to doll-face masks?" I suggested.

"Let's try it." He did as I said. The pages went down to only two.

We scrolled through various sites and finally narrowed the possibilities down to three different companies that created these masks.

"Chase, if we can find the company who made it, they can tell us who paid for it. It could lead us to the person who's behind this."

He nodded. "I think you're right. Let me make some phone calls and see what I can find out."

Just as he picked up his phone, someone knocked at

the door. He motioned for me to stay where I was as he went to answer.

Jamie burst into the house, a wide grin on her face. I'd told her I was here. "Guess what?"

I stood, anticipating where she was going with this. "What?"

"I'm engaged!"

CHAPTER FIFTEEN

I RUSHED toward her and glanced at her outstretched hand. A diamond ring sat on her finger, sparkling in the light.

"Oh, Jamie! Congratulations!" I pulled her into a hug, and we both squealed together.

Chase gave us our moment.

When we finally took a breath, he stretched out his arm for a congratulatory handshake. "I'm really happy for you and Wesley, Jamie. Congrats."

She beamed from ear to ear. "Thank you."

"How did he propose?" I held onto her arm, wanting to know every detail.

"He made me this wonderful dinner at his place, and then we went out to the overlook to see the city lights. One minute, I was staring at Cincinnati. The next minute, I turned around and he was on one knee." She squealed again. "I can't believe I'm getting married! You have to be my maid of honor."

"Of course. I'd love to be!"

Jamie and I stayed up for the next two hours talking about weddings and love. Chase disappeared, giving us some time to chat. I had a feeling he was making some phone calls about those masks. I really hoped that something turned up.

Just before midnight, Jamie went home. I reminded myself that I was a big girl and perfectly capable of making wise choices and utilizing self-control. Still, a flutter of nerves went through me. What if this wasn't a good idea?

Though I tried my best to forget about Chase's utterance of "I love you," it again fluttered into my mind. I would like nothing more than to believe his words had been true . . . but I couldn't let myself go there. I needed boundaries up in order to protect my heart.

As soon as Jamie left, Chase joined me on the couch, his eyes bright as he nodded toward the door. "Good news, huh? Your best friend is getting married."

I smiled. "Yeah, it is, isn't it? I'm really happy for her. She deserves all the happiness in the world."

"Her engagement is good news." He shifted, signaling a change in the conversation. "But I have other good news, as well. We tracked down the address of the man who ordered the mask. It's not far from here."

My breath caught. "Is that right?"

"Wilson is headed there now."

"Can we go?"

He took a step back, his face clouding. "That's not a good idea."

"What if I stay in the car? The whole time? I just want to know if it's him. I know you do too."

"I do but . . ."

"Please?"

Finally, he nodded. "Okay. Let's go."

———

CHASE and I drove across town to the condo that had been rented by someone named Tyler Billings. The police were still looking into him, but he appeared to be the person who'd ordered that mask.

I prayed we'd find the guy. That we'd stop him before he could do more damage.

Twenty minutes later, we pulled to a stop in front of an expensive condo complex that overlooked the Ohio River. The building was newer, with a contemporary design and neatly landscaped green spaces.

Chase left me in the car while he went over to chat with Wilson for a minute. I anxiously waited for him to return with news. Finally, ten minutes later, he did.

He climbed back into the driver's seat. "No one is there, but they got a warrant to search the place for clues. We should wait here for now."

"Understood." Silence fell in the car.

I stared out the window. Tapped my fingers. Tried to be patient.

Chase shifted, turning toward me. As I glanced at him, I saw the serious look in his eyes. He was about to say something either heartfelt or heart-crushing. I wasn't sure which.

Chase swallowed hard before saying, "I've missed you, Holly."

I blinked. Had I just heard him correctly? I knew I had, but his words threw me off balance. "I've missed you too, Chase."

"There's something I want you to know." He turned toward me in the vehicle.

I shifted in my seat so I could see him better. "What's that?"

"I've been going to a therapist the past few months."

I squinted, unsure if I'd heard him correctly. "What? Really?"

He glanced down at his hands before nodding. "Really. I know when we broke up, I said it was because I needed to deal with my brother and what happened to him. But I began to realize that I might not ever know what happened to him. I began to ask myself if I would be able to accept that."

"And?" I nearly held my breath as I waited for his response. This could be a major turning point in his emotional closure.

"And my therapist has been working with me and helping me realize that I can't change the past."

"What do you mean? What do you want to change?"

Chase shrugged. "I didn't realize the pressure I was putting on myself. The guilt I was bearing. I thought if I could find his killer that everything would right itself in my world. He's made me realize that it's not that simple."

"Life rarely is."

Chase glanced up at me, regret in his gaze. "I also came to realize what a mistake it was to let you walk away instead of fighting for our future together."

My heart skipped a beat. "Is that right?"

"You're the best thing that's ever happened to me, Holly. You make my world a better place. But I'm not sure you can say the same for me."

"Of course you made my life better. You make me feel safe, and you make me feel loved, and you accept me for who I am—even with all my quirks."

The corner of his lip curled. "You do have a lot of quirks."

Another moment of silence stretched. I knew there was something on my mind that I needed to tell him, despite the fear that made me want to remain quiet—to stay safe.

"I officially called things off with Drew, Chase."

Something flashed in his eyes. "Did you?"

"I've always known that the heart is deceitful. That

all the advice you ever hear about following your heart is wrong. So I thought I should take it in the opposite direction and follow my head. But the truth is that intellect isn't superior either."

Chase leaned closer. "Then what is?"

"A mix of both. But mostly trying to follow God's leading in your life. Sometimes it can be hard to separate all of those things."

"Tell me about it." He let out a short laugh before reaching toward me, before skimming his thumb over my cheek. I closed my eyes and leaned into his touch, relishing it.

"Holly, I—"

But before he could finish his sentence, someone tapped on the window.

Wilson.

My heart sank. Our conversation would have to be continued later.

Until then, I hoped Wilson had some good news to share with us.

CHAPTER SIXTEEN

CHASE ROLLED DOWN HIS WINDOW, and we waited to hear what Wilson had to say.

"This appears to be Tyler Billings' house," Wilson started. "And Tyler Billings appears to be just the person we're looking for."

"Did you find anything inside?" Chase asked. "Anything that will give us a clue about what he's planning? Where he is?"

"We're still combing through everything. We'll also talk to the neighbors. But we did find two custom masks inside."

I swallowed hard, not missing the "s" at the end of that last word. "He has more than one of that doll face?"

Wilson nodded and threw back a handful of Tic Tacs. "He does. In fact, the company said he ordered eight of them all together."

"Good to know." That meant the man could still appear in my life again. That he could still terrorize me.

Wilson pulled up something on his phone and showed me a picture of a man in his thirties with blond hair. He wore a suit and a bow tie. "Do you recognize this man?"

I shook my head, hoping for a spark of familiarity, but there wasn't any. "Not in the least."

Wilson nodded slowly before putting his phone away. "Okay."

"Do you know anything else about him?" Chase asked.

"He's an attorney. Seems well-respected in the area. I didn't find anything suggestive or controversial in his background."

"Why would this guy target me?" I asked. "Am I just a random victim?"

"That's a great question," Wilson said. "Are you random?"

His question resonated in my head. Was I random? Or had I been chosen for some reason?

I'd guess I'd been chosen. There'd been too much planning involved. But why? Why would this guy go through all this effort to make my life miserable? That's what didn't make sense.

Had I done something to him? Was this revenge? Was this somehow connected with a past crime I'd helped to solve?

My head pounded. Nothing was falling into place.

———

BACK AT THE HOUSE, Chase and I excused ourselves to our separate bedrooms. We were both tired, and the news that this guy had gotten away did nothing for our spirits.

But after lying in bed for thirty minutes, I couldn't sleep at all.

Finally, I threw my legs out of bed. Maybe some water would help.

After tugging my robe on, I sneaked from the room, down the hall, and into the kitchen.

I stopped in my tracks when I saw a shadow in the room.

"Holly?"

I released the air from my lungs. "Chase?"

He stepped close enough that I could see him, despite the darkness around us. It was definitely Chase. He wore an old T-shirt and some shorts and held a glass in his hands.

"What are you doing up?" I asked.

"I was thirsty. And I couldn't sleep."

"Me too. On both counts."

He handed me his glass. "Here. I'll get another one."

As he stepped away, I took a sip. But, even after drinking it, part of me still didn't feel satisfied.

I remembered our earlier conversation in the car, the one that had been cut short when Wilson came to the window. What was Chase about to say? There was so much that still needed to be voiced aloud.

If I were honest with myself, I'd admit that something had been stirring inside me over the past few days. Good or bad, it was the truth. I was going to have to figure out how to deal with that.

I watched as Chase poured some water into a glass, took a drink, and placed his glass on the counter. A moment later, he sauntered back over to where I stood.

As we faced each other, the darkness surrounding us, my heart beat out of control. I could tell that Chase was feeling the same things I was. The tension between us felt real enough to touch.

The next moment, we were in each other's arms. Chase gazed down at me, emotion welling in his eyes. He skimmed his fingers along my face, my neck, my lips.

My throat burned at his closeness, as memories from the past filled my heart.

Had I ever stopped loving Chase? I didn't think so. And I probably never would.

The next instant, his lips covered mine. Completely. Wholly. Without apology.

I was swept away into another world—a world without problems and worries and fears. A world where all that mattered was this moment. Chase and me.

Fire shot down my spine, the warmth sending delight through me. I'd missed this. I'd missed Chase. Missed the connection I felt with him.

As he pulled back, his hands grasped both sides of my face and he stared into my eyes. "Holly, when I realized that something was wrong and that you were missing, I thought I was going to go crazy. I had no doubt in my mind at that moment that you were the only woman for me. That I didn't want to go another day without you. That you were my soulmate."

Tears of joy pressed at my eyes. "Really?"

"Really." He smiled down at me, his gaze soft. "I love you, Holly Anna Paladin. I always have."

"Oh, Chase." Air left my lungs in a whoosh. "I love you too."

Without saying anything else, his lips met mine again. Softly. Tenderly. But with growing passion.

Chase finally pulled away and backed up a few steps. "We should probably call it a night."

He looked flushed, winded almost. In other words, he looked exactly how I felt.

We both stepped back from each other, as if we didn't trust ourselves.

Good idea.

"Yes, we should." I ran a hand through my hair. "We'll talk more. In the morning."

Chase nodded slowly, his gaze locked on mine. "That's a great idea. In the morning."

With one last glance at him, I scurried down the hallway to my room.

Chase and I . . . were we really an item again? Why did that thought both thrill me and scare me at the same time?

CHAPTER SEVENTEEN

I TRIED NOT to look giddy as I stared at Chase over the breakfast table the next morning. Jamie had stopped by —she'd actually left her wallet here—and she'd ended up eating breakfast with us. I'd felt more like myself, and fixed a bacon and cheese quiche.

My friend sat between us, and I noticed her gaze swinging back and forth from Chase to me, an eyebrow quirked.

She clearly knew something was up.

"Is there something you want to tell me?" she finally blurted. "Because you two keep giving each other googly eyes this morning."

"What?" I pushed my hair behind my ears and hid my smile. "No, we're not."

"I don't know what you're talking about," Chase said at the same time.

She let out a sassy *um-hm* and continued to eat her quiche—thankfully, I'd made a gluten-free version, so she could indulge with us. "It's about time you two got back together."

"Who said we're back together?" I asked, taking a sip of my coffee.

"It's obvious. It's been obvious from the start that you two would end up together. I was just waiting for everything to play out in the good Lord's timing. Can I get an amen?"

Chase and I exchanged a smile.

"Now that no one is pretending anymore, I just want to say I'm really happy for you," Jamie continued.

"Thank you . . ." My voice was tinged with uncertainty on how to respond to that.

"Now, what are you two doing today?" she asked. "Besides making googly eyes at each other."

I glanced at Chase. I really didn't know—other than realizing I needed to check on Kari again. I also wanted to verify parts of her story, but I wasn't sure I'd have time to do that today. Of course, I was desperately hoping for a breakthrough in the case.

I wanted to talk to Kari about the man she'd been seen with. I also wanted to follow up on Perry, the man who'd come into my office. Had anyone ever confirmed that he was truly out of town during all this?

I had so much to process and comprehend. The good news was that my boss was also my brother, and he understood why I couldn't go back to work yet. Though I knew I'd have piles of paperwork on my desk when I returned, it could wait. For now.

"I'll be following up some case leads," Chase said. "I'll be working, just not in the office."

Again, he was rearranging everything for me. I hated that this had turned his life upside down, and, despite my logic, I felt responsible.

I pushed the thoughts aside and cleared my throat. "Any updates you can share?"

He leaned back and looked at a paper. "Actually, yes. Kurt Casey . . . we've been looking into him some more. One of his best friends said Kurt had received some threats before he died."

"What?" The word left my lips in a gasp.

"He made some bad deals, hoping to get enough money to keep himself afloat. Unfortunately, some of them weren't legal. Someone found out about it and threatened to expose him if he didn't pay up to the tune of 500K."

"That's a big chunk of change—especially for someone having financial problems."

"Exactly."

"So he could have killed himself to avoid the scandal or . . ."

"Someone else could have killed him for not cooperating."

I leaned back. "Is this connected with the blackmail

of my brother's friend? I mean, two people in the same city being blackmailed at the same time . . . is that a coincidence?"

"I haven't seen any signs that the two cases are connected. But I can't rule it out either."

I shook my head, trying to let all of that sink in. "Man, who would have thought?"

"People will do whatever they can to make some money." Chase studied me a moment. "And, Holly, never think you're an inconvenience."

My cheeks flushed at his sweet words. "Why would you say that?"

"Because I can read the guilt on your face. I'm doing all this because I want to, not because I feel obligated."

"And there you guys go again, sounding all sappy," Jamie crooned with a playful eye roll.

She was acting annoyed, but I could tell she really was happy. I knew my friend only wanted what was best for me. Besides, she was engaged now.

"Well, I have to go to work," Jamie stood, plate in hand. "So I'll leave you two be. Behave yourselves."

"We will," I called.

But as she left, leaving Chase and I alone, I nearly felt giddy. As I put my plate in the sink, he stepped up behind me and put his arms around my waist. I turned until I saw his face, until I saw the smoky look in his eyes.

RANDOM ACTS OF INIQUITY   153

He leaned down and kissed me, and I knew I was in trouble.

Any man who made my toes curl like this was trouble.

Before the kiss could deepen, Chase's cell phone rang. He stepped back with an apologetic shrug and put the phone to his ear. "Hey, Wilson. What's going on?"

He muttered a few more things into the phone before ending the call and sliding the phone back into his pocket.

"What is it?"

"Apparently, they brought in an IT guy who works for a taskforce run by the state police. This guy found something on your computer, and Wilson wants us to come in so we can talk about it."

My breath caught. "He didn't say what it was?"

"No, no clues even."

I nibbled on my bottom lip. "Interesting."

"Let's go. I know you want to check on Kari on the way out." He grabbed his keys from the table.

"That would be great."

"Let's get moving then."

———

AS I CLIMBED out of Chase's car at the motel, I glanced around. I didn't see anyone watching us. But, despite my giddiness at the turn in my relationship with Chase, the bigger issue right now was the man intent on making me miserable.

He was doing a fine job. I felt the continual need to look over my shoulder. I kept expecting another phone call from someone to inform me they'd gotten a message from my phone that I hadn't sent. I waited to see another video taken of myself unaware.

The whole thing didn't make any sense. I had no idea why someone would do something like this. Why they would target me.

Sometimes, not knowing was the worst part.

It was gray outside today and drizzling. Plus, the wind seemed to have shifted and brought with it a chill. I'd only packed a sweater for myself, but I pulled it around me, trying to stay warm, as I stepped up to Kari's room and knocked at the door.

I waited several minutes, but there was no answer.

"Maybe she's in the shower," I suggested.

"Maybe." But the frown on Chase's face showed what he really thought.

He hadn't been a fan of me helping Kari. He thought she was a con artist. Truth was, he could be right. But I'd rather believe the best in people and be hurt than to let my heart be hardened and become suspicious of everyone.

I knocked again.

There was still no answer.

I paced over to the window and tried to peer

between the opening in the curtains, but it was no use. I couldn't see anything.

I nibbled on my bottom lip, trying to figure out the next step.

"What do you want to do?" Chase turned toward me.

There was only one thing I could think of to do. I grabbed the knob and twisted it.

To my surprise, the door wasn't latched.

Chase and I exchanged a look.

He nudged me back and drew his gun. "Let me go first."

I remained close to him as he stepped inside. I tried to see how the room looked, but I couldn't see over Chase's broad shoulders.

"Hello?" He cautiously took another step.

No response. No sound of the water running.

Once I was able to, I shifted from behind Chase and scanned the room. The bed was made. Everything appeared in order . . . almost like Kari had never been here.

My stomach knotted, but I tried not to play the "what if" scenario reel in my mind.

"Kari?" Chase continued, stepping into the center of the room.

Still, no answer.

Where had she gone? Maybe she'd just run to get some breakfast. That seemed the best-case scenario.

But as I followed Chase toward the bathroom, I nearly collided with him. He paused and peered down at the floor between the bed and the wall.

I sucked in a deep breath.

Blood. There was a puddle of blood there on the carpet.

I closed my eyes.

What had happened to Kari?

CHAPTER EIGHTEEN

WILSON and his team had come to the hotel and scoured Kari's room. They'd taken a sample of the blood and would send it off for testing. They'd also questioned everyone nearby, and no one had seen anything.

It appeared that Kari had disappeared into thin air again.

I crossed my arms and leaned against the rough brick exterior of the motel, staying beneath the overhang to avoid the cool drizzle of rain that had started to fall. Maybe I should never have left Kari alone. I'd never considered that she might be in danger.

Chase stepped from the hotel room and found me. His gaze indicated he was practically reading my thoughts right now—reading the guilt and the way I was beating myself up.

"You couldn't have known." Chase stood beside me a moment, studying my expression with worry.

"I know. But I still feel I should have done more."

"I'd say you already went above and beyond."

"I just don't understand, Chase. Was she involved in this? Or is she a victim?"

"Given her history—which has included a lot of lies—it's really hard to say. Wilson and his men will look for her."

I nodded, even though I didn't know if I believed him.

Across the parking lot, I spotted a woman peeking out of her motel door. No doubt she was wondering what the commotion was about. But what if she knew more?

"Did Wilson talk to her?" I nodded toward the woman.

Chase followed my gaze. The woman saw him looking at her and slipped inside the room, closing the door. "I don't think so. They didn't hit every room."

"I'd like to see if she'll talk to me."

"Let's give it a shot."

We hurried down the sidewalk to her door and pounded on the wood frame. She didn't answer.

I tried again.

Little did this woman know that I wasn't one to give up.

When there was still no answer, I leaned close to the

door and said loudly, "Please, I have some questions for you. My cousin was staying in that hotel room where the police are. I need to know if you saw anything. Please."

It felt weird to call Kari my cousin. But we were related, and, if her story was true, we were cousins. It seemed the easiest explanation at the moment.

I waited. Hoped. Prayed.

A moment later, I heard something jangle on the other side of the door. The locks slid and turned until finally the door opened. The woman peeked out, her pale face looking dazed.

"What do you want?" the woman whispered.

Behind her, I heard a TV on and some other commotion. What exactly was going on in there?

"I don't want trouble," I started. "I just need to know if you saw anything."

She stared at me, her eyes wide and scared. Her gaze darted beyond me to the police then to Chase. "I just try to mind my own business."

Something about the way the woman said the words, about the way she was dressed, and the little bit of the hotel room I could see behind her, made me think she lived here permanently.

Another sound caught my ear. A little laugh.

There were kids inside the hotel room, I realized. I'd seen more than my fair share of situations like this as a social worker. Sometimes, people didn't have the proper credit to get a house or apartment. So they rented day by day or week by week at establishments like this. It wasn't ideal, but at least they had a roof over their heads until they could get back on their feet.

"Did you see something over at that room?" I asked, pointing. "Please. It's important. Anything will help."

Her gaze darted to the room again before turning back to me. "I thought I heard a scream this morning. I peeked out the curtain. Honestly, I hear a lot of things around here. A nice car was in the parking lot—not like the kind that are usually around here. The next thing I saw was a man come out of that room. He had his arms around a woman, and he led her to his car."

I swallowed hard at the image. "She was upset?"

"She seemed to be. She looked like she was crying."

"But she was alive," I muttered, more for myself than anyone else. I needed confirmation.

The woman recoiled, as if the question shocked her. "Yes, she was alive. They got in the car, and the man drove away."

"Did he force her into the vehicle?" Chase asked.

"I . . . I don't know. He stood close to her. But she wasn't kicking and screaming. It's hard to say."

"Can you describe the man?" Chase asked, using a softer than usual voice, probably in an effort not to scare the woman.

It didn't work. She seemed to shrivel back as soon as Chase spoke.

"It's okay," I said. "He's with me. He's one of the good guys."

I'd learned that not everyone trusted the police. Some people saw them as avengers who took their children away, who followed the law at the cost of serving the people. Sometimes, police work wasn't well received, especially in poorer communities.

The woman pulled her gaze away from Chase and back to me. "It's hard to say. He was far away. He wore a black hoodie."

My stomach dropped with disappointment. "What about his car? What was he driving?"

"It was also black. Like I said, it looked expensive. I don't know what kind it was, though."

"You didn't by chance see the license plate, did you?" I asked.

"Only the first three letters. AN3."

I glanced at Chase. It was something. I'd take that over nothing.

And at least we knew that Kari was still alive when she left her hotel room.

———

CHASE and I went back to the station. We met with Wilson in his office, and I'd nearly forgotten that the detective had said they'd discovered something on my laptop. All I'd been thinking about was Kari.

"There are a few things I want to ask you about, Ms. Paladin," Wilson said as we sat in his cramped office.

"Okay. What's going on?" A strange flutter of nerves went crazy inside me. Chase sat beside me, waiting to hear the update also. I figured it was big if he'd called us in to talk face-to-face.

"As this guy from the state police-appointed task-force was looking through your computer, trying to figure out how this guy was able to access it so easily, we came across some online searches you'd done that made us curious."

The flutters in my stomach grew larger. I'd searched for a lot of crazy stuff. I'd stuck my nose in many places I shouldn't have. But I had no idea which particular thing he was talking about.

"What was that?" I asked.

"It appears you were doing some research on a company called Axon Enterprises."

My stomach dropped as I realized where he was going with this.

I glanced at Chase, starting to explain but realizing I didn't know what to say.

"That was the company my brother worked for." Surprise laced Chase's voice.

"I know—"

"You were still looking into his death?" His surprise turned into accusation as he turned toward me.

He'd asked me to stay out of it. The subject had been

one of our many fights. Whatever world Hayden had been involved with, Chase wanted me to stay far away from it. But I hadn't listened.

"I can explain. It's not like it sounds." I felt things going south and knew I needed to quickly correct them before this misunderstanding led to something unsalvageable.

"I'll let you two talk about that later." Wilson looked like he didn't want to be in the middle of any drama. "I need to know what you were looking into exactly."

I shifted in my seat, wishing I could disappear. But I couldn't. I had to face this and hope that I could make things right with Chase later. But my stomach churned with unease.

I turned back to Wilson. "How is this important to this investigation? That search was just something I was doing in my free time, a way of trying to find answers."

His lip twitched, as if he didn't like being questioned. "It turns out the IP address of that website is linked to the IP address of whoever accessed your camera."

The pit in my stomach grew deeper as connections began forming in my mind. This couldn't all go back to that . . . could it?

"So?" Wilson shook something in his pocket—probably a container of orange-colored candy, if I had to guess.

I could feel his patience waning.

I turned my gaze away from Chase. There was no need to deny what I'd done. "Yes, I was looking into Axon. As you probably know, they shut down a couple of years ago."

"That's correct. They were a tech company."

I nodded nervously. "Yes."

"What exactly did you find out, Ms. Paladin?"

I rubbed my hands on my jeans, trying to ward away my anxiety. "About a month ago, I found a woman who used to work for them named Barbara Jostens."

"I talked to Barbara after my brother's death." Chase's voice went from outraged to just plain disappointed.

The disappointment felt harder to swallow than anger.

I licked my lips before continuing. "Yes, I know. But when you talked to her, it was fresh after your brother's death. It's been six years now."

"What difference did it make?" Chase asked.

"A lot of time has passed," I said. "Barbara seemed a little more willing to talk. I suppose an armchair detective with a penchant for wearing dresses isn't as intimidating as a former pro football player turned detective who's angry about his brother's death. I was supposed to meet her two weeks ago."

"Two weeks ago? Were you not going to tell me about this?" Chase's eyes probed mine, searching for the truth.

"Detective, we need to stay focused," Wilson said.

Chase looked away before letting out a long breath. "Of course."

I glanced at my lap, trying to pull my thoughts together. "It didn't matter. Barbara chickened out. She didn't meet me, nor did she answer any more of my phone calls. I was disappointed because she'd seemed excited to talk to me. In fact, she said she hoped that someone would come knocking again because she had information she wanted to share."

Wilson typed a few things into his computer. As he stared at the screen, his lips pulled down in a frown. "The Louisville Police found her dead in her home."

He showed us a police report that he must have just pulled up.

"She was shot in an apparent home invasion," Wilson continued.

I glanced at Chase. His bottom lip dropped. He obviously didn't know either. Then again, he probably hadn't been following Barbara. At least not recently.

I shook my head, willing my thoughts to be wrong. "So . . . you're saying that Axon might be somehow connected with what happened to me? That maybe that was the domino that got knocked down and set all this in motion? All because of something I was looking into?"

Wilson offered a grim nod. "That's what we're wondering."

Chase shook his head and looked at me, displeasure evident in his frown. "I told you to stay out of it."

"I know but—" Panic surged in me. This was not the way things were supposed to play out.

Chase stood and paced toward the door, his muscles clearly tense and stiff. "Not now, Holly."

I clamped my mouth shut.

"Detective Dexter," another man said. "We have a follow-up on another case you're working. It needs a minute of your time."

Chase gave me one last look before walking away.

As he disappeared from sight, my shoulders drooped. We'd gotten back together just in time for me to screw things up. Would Chase even listen to my side of things?

I had no idea.

But I felt horrible. And I wasn't sure I'd be able to fix this.

CHAPTER NINETEEN

WILSON GLANCED AT ME. Was that pity in his gaze? Maybe. But I knew this wasn't the time to address it, nor did I want him to feel the need to act as my therapist. Instead, I let out a deep breath, unsure what exactly to do with myself at the moment.

I hated the awkwardness in the room. Hated the flash of shame and embarrassment I felt.

Wilson shifted, almost like he was going to pretend the terse exchange hadn't happened. "Walk me through what you know about Axon."

I nodded, grateful for something to focus on other than my downfalls. I wiped my palms on my jeans and drew in a deep breath. "They were an email marketing group based out of Louisville, Kentucky. Chase's brother, Hayden, worked for them for about six months."

"What did Hayden do?"

"He handled security at the front entrance. I guess they'd gotten some threats and felt the need to hire someone to keep an eye on things. Hayden had been a bouncer at a club in town before that. He didn't have much 'official' experience, but he was brawny and intimidating, from what I hear." I'd found that out partially through Chase and partly through my own research.

"Tell me again what happened to him. How did he die?"

"He was badly beaten and killed by a single bullet through the heart about six years ago. His killer has never been found, although a man with the first name of Hugo had been suspected of his death."

"There was no other evidence to indicate motive or any background on the crime?"

"Not as far as I know. Hayden was jogging through a park at night when he was beaten and shot." Chase had told me that much.

"And Hayden was Chase's younger brother? What was their relationship like?" Wilson squinted as he tried to put the pieces together.

"He was his half-brother, although they'd only met about a year before Hayden died. Chase's father left the family when Chase was young. He ran off and started a new life, apparently. Chase had no idea he even had a brother."

"And this turned Chase's life upside down, I imagine?"

I frowned as I remembered hearing Chase talk about it. "Yes. He was thrilled to discover he had a brother, then Hayden was snatched away. It was difficult. He has had no real family since his mom died. His dad was . . . absent, to say the least."

"Did you know him during that time?"

I was beginning to feel like I was being interrogated with these rapid-fire questions. I also felt like Chase should be here to answer them instead of me. But I supposed, at this point, it was more about my involvement in the investigation than it was about Chase's brother.

"No, we hadn't reconnected when that happened," I said. "He was still playing professional football."

"I see." Wilson nodded slowly, thoughtfully.

I studied the detective a moment, trying to figure out where he was going with all these questions. "What are you thinking?"

"I'm just trying to piece this puzzle together. You started researching Hayden's death, which in turn means you researched Axon. When did you start focusing on the company?"

"Probably a month or two ago."

He nodded slowly, thoughtfully. "So, maybe about that same time, this plan was set in place to abduct you and set you up in a retro-style house. Is that a connection? That's what we need to figure out."

"I'd like to figure that out also."

"Two people who could be connected are already dead here . . . Kurt Casey and Barbara Jostens. This isn't just a game. It's a deadly game. Maybe the answers can be found in some of these searches you did on your computer. Maybe you stumbled into something you shouldn't have."

"It's an idea worth exploring."

Wilson turned back to my laptop and hit a few keys. He straightened and frowned as he stared at the computer screen. The next instant, he began tapping some keys.

"What's wrong?" I stood, trying to get a better look.

He didn't answer. Instead, he grabbed his phone and punched in a number. "I need you in here. Now. Something's happening."

Just as the words left his lips, the lights in the building flickered.

My stomach clenched.

Power surge? Or was this a tech genius at work, disrupting the computer, the lights, and who knew what else?

————

THE MAN from the taskforce rushed into the room. I'd

been introduced to him earlier. Felix, I believe was his name. Wilson had said he'd be my new best friend.

The man was tall, with chunky glasses, a blue baseball cap, and an uptight expression. He stared at my computer and kept hitting keys while muttering things under his breath.

He practically shoved Wilson out of the way and took his seat at the computer. Wilson remained behind the desk, watching the tech's every move.

"I don't know what's happened." Felix's fingers raced across the keyboard. "It appears someone has hacked into the system and is deleting all the files from this computer. I've got to get this offline."

He unplugged it then continued to furiously type.

I'd backed up most of my files to the cloud, and I hoped they were safe there. Besides, other concerns seemed more pressing than me losing all my photos.

Had we come too close to discovering something important? That was the only thing that made sense to me. Why else would someone be wiping my computer clean right now? How was this even possible?

Chase charged into the room amidst the flickering lights and a nervous murmur throughout the room. "Is everything okay?"

"We don't know what's going on." Wilson scowled at the computer. "Whoever is behind all of this has a wicked sense of humor."

"Why would you say that?" Chase glanced at Felix and Wilson.

It didn't go unnoticed that he avoided my gaze.

"Someone is erasing documents from the computer, almost like he knows we're getting closer to him and wants to destroy any evidence," Felix said.

"Speaking of which, I just got another update," Chase started. "Tyler Billings was involved in an auto accident four days ago. He's in the hospital still. He doesn't appear to be the person behind this. Whoever ordered those masks must have known Billings was in the hospital. Doll Man could have picked up the masks at the front door while Billings was laid up in a coma."

"But there were masks inside," Wilson said.

Chase shrugged. "Maybe this guy planted them there."

Wilson muttered something under his breath and seemed to chew on the thought for a minute. "So this was just a smokescreen? A way to throw us off his trail again?"

Chase shrugged, his face appearing tense and his expression stormy. "That's how it appears."

I nibbled at the inside of my mouth, fighting discouragement.

This person was always two steps ahead of us. Always.

How was that?

I didn't know. But I didn't like it.

CHAPTER TWENTY

CHASE WENT BACK to researching Tyler Billings more and looking for any possible connections that might lead us to the real bad guy. He'd barely glanced at me, and I knew I needed to give him time.

As I sat in the chair in the office, lights flickering above me, I closed my eyes. I'd love nothing more than to go home, but I knew I couldn't. Since I was trapped here at the station, I decided to review everything I knew.

A man had abducted me. He had to have been planning it for several weeks in advance. Maybe he'd been watching me in the process, and those were the eyes I'd felt on me.

Somehow, he'd known I loved all things retro. He must have seen the article on developer Kurt Casey and decided the model home in the new neighborhood would be an ideal place to hold me captive. For some reason, this guy had killed Kurt and made it look like a suicide. That was my theory, at least.

Before he'd grabbed me, he'd had enough forethought to install cameras and microphones. He'd also put enough thought into this to steal Tyler Billings' identity and order the creepy masks on his account, even get it sent to this other guy's address.

What about the auto accident Tyler had been in? Was it truly an accident, and had the man just capitalized on it? Or had the man who'd abducted me somehow caused the accident?

Then came the twist that made me the most uncomfortable. I'd tried to get in contact with Barbara Jostens. Two weeks later, she turned up dead.

Two weeks ago was when I started feeling like someone was watching me. Coincidence? I had a hard time believing that.

What if this *was* all connected? What had Barbara known that had been worth killing over? Would I ever find out?

And what about Kari Leblanc? Was she innocent in this whole scheme? Had she told me the truth about her connection to me? Or was she somehow involved? Who was the man she'd been spotted with? Where had that blood come from? And where had she gone with the man in the expensive black car?

My head pounded. Nothing made sense. Nothing at all. I had too many questions and not enough answers.

And now my nosiness appeared to be ruining my newly rekindled relationship with Chase. Would I ever have the chance to tell him that I'd only looked into Hayden's death as a way of trying to help him? I'd wanted him to have closure. It wasn't about me or even about the two of us. It was about helping someone I cared about. But maybe I should have minded my own business. Chase had asked me to do that, and I hadn't.

Someone else appeared at the door, this time a younger woman wearing a police uniform. "Excuse me, I'm looking for a Holly Anna Paladin."

I scrunched my eyebrows together in confusion before waving half-heartedly. Most people didn't look for me at the police station. "That's me."

"Ms. Paladin, there's someone here to see you."

I pointed to myself, still uncertain I'd heard her correctly. "To see me?"

Who in the world knew I was here?

"That's correct," the woman said. "He says it's important."

First, someone had sent Jamie here under the guise of an emergency. Now, someone else had been sent here?

I didn't like how much this guy knew about my schedule and my whereabouts. But I was really curious about who wanted to see me.

A FEW MINUTES LATER, a man with a partially bald head and the beginnings of a pudgy belly stepped into the doorway.

I'd never seen him before. He didn't appear dangerous—he looked too out of shape for that.

His gaze fell on me. "Holly, I'm so glad you're here."

I stood, surprised that he'd recognized me. "And you are?"

He twisted his head as if confused. "I'm Mitch Kendrick."

I shook my head, the name not ringing any bells. There was something major I was missing here, and I had no idea what.

"We've been texting." He leaned forward and talked slowly, as if I had issues.

Realization hit me. I knew that Doll Man had sent texts on my behalf, but was he also intercepting my texts? And how did he know I was at the station right now?

My insides turned to ice—crackling cold ice.

I glanced at Wilson, who looked as concerned as I felt. He downed another handful of Tic Tacs like a drug addict swallowing pills.

Felix, the tech guy, still sat behind the desk, tapping away at my computer but occasionally glancing up like he was anxious to hear what was going on also.

Just to be safe, I was going to play along with this. "Texting . . . that's right. But I feel like I've missed something."

"I'm not sure what there is to miss," Mitch started, moisture staining the shirt beneath his armpits. "I texted to see if we could meet. You said yes. I told you I was coming into town from Louisville today, and you said to come down to the station to talk."

Louisville? That's where Axon had been based and where Barbara had lived.

"Right." I nodded, hating the off-balance feeling swirling in my head. So he was connected somehow to Axon and Barbara, I would guess.

"I can't believe Barbara's dead." Mitch hung his head and his shoulders hunched with grief. "You're the only one who can help."

I sucked in a breath when he mentioned Barbara. As I observed his sadness.

Mitch was Barbara's boyfriend, wasn't he? It made sense.

I tried to search my memories. I'd looked at Barbara's social media profiles. There had been a man with her in her more recent pictures. I was pretty sure that man was Mitch. He'd been wearing a baseball cap, though, which covered his baldness.

Wilson moved around to the front of the desk and leaned against it, then pointed to the chair beside me. "Have a seat."

Mitch nervously lowered himself next to me, and I turned toward him, desperate for answers yet trying to play it cool—at least until we had more information.

"What brings you here, Mr. Kendrick?" Wilson asked.

"Barbara's death, of course." He sounded nearly winded as he sagged in the chair and ran a hand over his face. "Someone from that company she used to work for killed her. I just know it."

My heart pounded against my chest as I processed his words. "Why do you think that? Barbara hasn't worked for Axon in several years."

"I know. But she realized they were up to something, and she was tired of being quiet." He fanned his face. "Is it hot in here or is it just me?"

Wilson ignored his question. "I'm going to need to know what you know."

Mitch shook his head rapidly and pulled something out of his pocket. "Of course. It's all on here. Everything you need to bring that company down."

Wilson took the jump drive from him and handed it to Felix. "Do you have a secure computer where we can run this?"

The tech grabbed a laptop from a bag on the floor and booted it up. "My computer has all the safeguards in place that we should need. No one should be able to hack into it."

"Great," Wilson said. "Let's see what's on that jump drive."

The tech plugged it into his computer and tapped some keys. I could hardly breathe as I waited to find out what was on there. What kind of evidence did he have? Would it be something to close this case and point us to the real bad guy?

Part of me wanted to call Chase in here . . . then again, I knew we should wait. If this was nothing, I didn't want to get his hopes up. Plus, I still wasn't sure he wanted to see me.

My heart twisted at the conundrum. I really hoped the two of us could talk later. But right now, I'd deal with this issue.

Felix leaned closer to the screen. "It looks like Barbara had some official documents here from Axon."

"What do they imply?" Wilson asked.

The tech's lips twisted. "That's what I'm not sure about."

Wilson crossed to the other side of the desk so he could see them also.

"It looks like large amounts of money were being exchanged," Felix continued. "I'm just not sure if this was on or off the books."

"Can we print the files and pour over them?" Wilson said. "There's got to be something to this. Maybe it's the link we've been looking for."

"Absolutely." Felix sucked in a quick breath, his eyes fastened to the screen. "Wait . . . "

"What's wrong?" I asked, almost not wanting to know.

"The files . . ." Felix muttered. "They're being deleted as we speak. I don't think I can stop it."

CHAPTER TWENTY-ONE

"WHAT?" Wilson leaned toward the desk, his eyes narrowing.

Felix typed furiously, his face reddening as his gaze intensified. "This shouldn't be happening, not on this computer."

"Can't you stop it?" Wilson asked.

Felix grabbed the cord that connected his computer to the system. "I'm trying to stop it. But it appears the jump drive may have set off a virus in my computer."

The man's fingers moved so quickly that I could practically see steam coming from them. He seemed to be doing everything in his power to stop this. Would it be enough?

Please don't let the files disappear. Please.

I glanced at Mitch. His face had gone pale also, but he said nothing, only waited.

Finally, Felix leaned back and shook his head as he stared at the computer screen. "It's gone."

"All of the files?" My voice came out as a high-pitched squeak. I couldn't believe it. The evidence had just been there. We'd done the right thing and opened it on a safe computer with an experienced tech.

"I don't know who these people are behind this," Felix said. "But I've never seen anyone so brilliant. There's no way he should have gotten through this firewall. No way."

Wilson sagged against the desk, looking weary. This case was taking its toll on everyone. "Mr. Kendrick, do you have any idea what was on that jump drive?"

He shrugged. "I have to admit that I did look at it."

My breath caught. Maybe all wasn't lost. "And?"

"And I can tell you what I think, based on what Barbara told me." Mitch swung his gaze from Wilson back to me, a hopeful look in his eyes.

Maybe this was finally it. The moment we would get some answers. I prayed that was the case.

Mitch ran his hand across his face again and drew in a deep breath. "Barbara got a job with Axon when they first opened," Mitch said. "The company specialized in internet marketing, with a lean toward email campaigns. Of course, the tech world has changed a lot since then, but they were cutting edge when they started."

"Go on," Wilson said, seeming to perk up just slightly.

"But, from what I gathered, Barbara began to sense that everything wasn't as it seemed with the company. She became increasingly unhappy. Finally, she quit. She couldn't do it anymore."

"What kind of illegal things were they doing?" Wilson downed some more Tic Tacs, looking like some Xanax might benefit him more.

Mitch shrugged. "I'm not 100 percent sure about it. But my impression is that they were exploiting people. They were hacking into people's private email accounts, finding information that could bring them down, and then threatening them with it."

More exploitation? This couldn't be a coincidence. Kurt Casey had been exploited also. And what about Ralph's friend?

I wanted to be appalled, but I wasn't really surprised. I glanced at Felix, trying to gauge his reaction. He didn't seem to be paying attention. His full focus was on the computer screen as his eyes rapidly went from left to right, as if reading something.

"Who were these people?" Wilson asked.

"They were powerful people. People with means and wealth. People who would pay out generously in order to protect their good name and their companies. We're talking politicians, business owners, sport stars."

The stakes were getting higher and more things were falling into place.

"If she was uncomfortable with what was happening, did she ever talk about taking it to the authorities?" I asked.

Mitch nodded and dabbed at the sweat-covered skin on his forehead. "She wanted to. But she was scared. Then she got some threats through email. The notes disappeared after she read them, leaving no evidence. Basically, these people were blackmailing her. They had set up all this evidence claiming that if she talked, they'd make her look just as guilty. It scared her."

"That's understandable." Wilson leaned against the wall, taking in every detail of the conversation.

"So she stayed quiet. She didn't know what else to do. She had a twelve-year-old son at home at the time. She had to think about him."

"So there was a lot on the line if Barbara went forward to the police with the information," I muttered.

"Exactly."

"Mr. Kendrick, why are you coming forward with this information now?" Wilson asked.

Mitch glanced at me. "Barbara told me you'd contacted her. She felt like maybe she was far enough removed from the company now that she could talk. Plus, her son is away at college. It's been eating her alive for years, and I think she was secretly hoping for a push, some encouragement to spill everything."

I held my breath as I waited for him to continue.

"She was all set and scheduled a meeting with you." Mitch's voice caught. "But then . . . she was killed. I still can't believe it. I knew I couldn't let her death be for nothing. I had to do something, so that's why I contacted you and came here. I want justice for Barbara."

———

GUILT POUNDED at me as I leaned back in my seat and squeezed my eyes shut. If I hadn't researched Axon and contacted Barbara, none of this would have happened. She would still be alive. Maybe other people would still be alive right now, and I wouldn't have gone through the trauma of being abducted.

All because I got curious and wanted to help give Chase closure—a fact that might lead to the demise of our relationship.

Think on the bright side, Holly. You must be getting close to answers. Close enough that someone felt threatened.

Was that what had set all of these events into motion?

I mean, it seemed like the founder of this company liked playing games with people.

Doll Man had definitely played games with me. Were these guys one and the same?

I didn't know, but my gut told me all of this was connected.

"What was the name of Axon's president?" Wilson asked.

"His name's Gerald Moven," Mitch said.

"Felix, see what you can find out on him." Wilson seemed to spring to life with a new energy as he stood. "I want to know where this guy is now."

"Yes, sir."

Wilson turned back to Mitch. "Is there anything else we need to know? Anything else you can remember?"

He shook his head and shrugged. "I . . . I don't know. Barbara didn't like to talk about it, but she thought there was enough evidence on that jump drive to bring this company down. She'd been sitting on it for years. She was going to give it to Holly."

I frowned, hoping desperately that Felix would be able to recover it. I wanted evidence and answers and closure. It seemed like Mitch was handing me all of those things.

"Can I ask you a question, Mitch?" I started, shifting my body toward him.

"Of course." He looked up at me, drops of sweat sprinkled across his face.

"Does the name Hayden Dexter ring any bells with you?"

He didn't hesitate before nodding. "Yes, Barbara talked about Hayden."

My breath caught. "What did she say?"

"From what I remembered, he acted as security for the company," Mitch said. "He stood by the front door, making sure there was no trouble."

"It's starting to make sense why they hired someone for that now," I said. "I used to think it sounded crazy, but if the guy running the company was dabbling in extortion, he'd probably need some protection."

"My understanding is that Hayden discovered what was really going on. At first, he took a cut of the money, but then he started to be bothered by it. He also tried to quit, but Gerald wouldn't let him."

"And you think that's ultimately why he died?" I asked.

Mitch nodded. "That's my theory."

"Wilson, I found what I could on this Gerald Moven guy." Felix turned his computer around to face us. "This is the picture that was online, but I can't find much more on him."

I blanched when I saw the picture.

"What is it?" Wilson asked. "You know this man?"

"That's the man who came into my office last week —the one who asked me out and who's supposedly visiting his mother on the West Coast. Perry Gutherson."

Wilson turned back to Mitch. "Is that what the man looked like who ran Axon?"

Mitch stared at the picture and shrugged. "I'm . . .

I'm not sure. I never saw him myself, I only heard his name."

Wilson began pacing the corner of his office. "So Perry Gutherson is really Gerald Moven."

"In theory, yes. But in reality, both of those names could be aliases," Felix said. "This guy seems to like setting up false identities. Who knows what name he's using now? It wouldn't surprise me if this wasn't his real picture either."

I nibbled on my bottom lip a moment. We'd come so far and had found out so much new information. But the truth was, we were still so far from finding answers.

Was Perry Gutherson really Gerald Moven? Was he behind all of this? And what would it take for us to find answers?

CHAPTER TWENTY-TWO

TWO HOURS LATER, Mitch had been sent to a hotel with police protection. Chase had been filled in on what was going on. Then we'd been sent home.

It was just as well. Nighttime had fallen. The air had turned chillier. And I couldn't deny that I was exhausted. My brain felt like it might explode, and rest could be just what I needed.

As Chase and I sat in his car together, driving to his place, tension wrangled the air. I knew he wasn't happy with me, but I didn't know what to say to fix it. So I let him have his space.

And I tried to accept the fact that just as we'd gotten back together, we might have ended again. The thought caused a sharp ache in my heart. I knew I couldn't undo what I'd done. I just had to wait for Chase to make up his mind as to whether or not he could accept me with all my flaws.

We pulled to a stop in front of his house, but Chase made no move to get out. Instead, he turned toward me, that same disappointed look in his eyes.

"I hardly know what to say, Holly."

I held back my tears. I hardly knew either. "Look, if you don't want me to stay here at your place, that's fine. I know you're mad."

He rubbed his lips together before saying, "It's not that I'm mad . . . it's just that I asked you not to get involved, and you did."

I wanted to make up excuses or deny it or defend myself, but sometimes, you just had to own your actions. "I did. We'd broken up, so I didn't think it mattered anymore. And I wasn't pursuing my unofficial 'investigation' on a regular basis. On occasion, I'd pop online and see what I could find out. I didn't really expect it to lead anywhere."

"But it did."

I frowned. "It did. I should have stayed out of it. But I didn't. And I can't change that now. I'm sorry, Chase."

"I love it that you're curious and passionate. I do. But I also need to know I can trust you."

I rubbed my fingers together, knowing his words had truth. When we'd broken up, he wasn't the only one with issues. I had my own. "You're right. I messed up."

His haggard gaze met mine, the depth of emotion there nearly haunting. "I don't want to lose you again."

"I don't want to lose you either, Chase." My voice cracked, revealing all the feelings I'd stuffed down inside.

He reached for me and planted a hard kiss on my lips. "I love you, Holly Anna Paladin."

A half smile, half cry captured my lips. "I love you too, Chase Dexter."

He let out a sigh and looked away, every movement looking like it took too much effort. "I'd love to enjoy this moment. To pretend like everything is great. To live a normal life. But you and I both know we have to figure out what's going on here first."

His words made sense. "Agreed. We should wait until this investigation is cleared up. Right now, we're not doing ourselves any favors by adding our emotions into the thick of things. We won't do this investigation justice if you and I keep getting in the way of it."

"Agreed," Chase said. "But . . . when this is all over, Holly? I want to talk. To really talk. To talk about moving forward, about our future."

My cheeks heated at the intensity of his words. "I'd like that."

He leaned back and let out a breath. "Okay, I'm going to change the topic now before I get sucked into talking about us. Don't get me wrong—I'd love to talk more, but—"

"I understand."

"So, back to the case." He paused, swallowed, and then continued, as if he needed to take a moment to compose himself and gather his thoughts. "There are a few things I don't understand. Hayden was killed because of what he knew. Barbara was also killed for what she knew. This guy—possibly Gerald Moven aka Perry Gutherson—discovered your connection, discovered that you were digging into this, and acted as though you could be a threat. But he didn't kill you."

"Strange, huh?" I'd thought about that also. "Maybe he wants to teach me a lesson? Use me as an example? Prove something? I have no idea."

"I don't either. And how does Kari tie into all of this?"

"Another good question. I have a hard time believing she's connected with the mess at Axon. But I do feel like she's connected in some way. It's all confusing, like a ball of yarn that's been jumbled together."

"We've got to start finding some answers soon." He took my hand. "Let's get inside. I asked Ralph to stop by. I have some questions about his friend. He said he was going to bring some food."

"That sounds like a plan."

But as we stepped into Chase's house a moment later, he froze and put a finger over his lips.

What was he doing?

As he began looking around, I realized the truth.

Chase thought someone had been here. Were they still here?

———

CHASE SWEPT the house but didn't find any hidden devices. It was only after every inch had been gone over that he finally spoke.

"Someone has been inside," he said.

I'd figured that, but just hearing the words out loud gave me chills. "How do you know?"

"I can sense it." He looked stiff as he continued to glance around the room. "There's something different, I just can't figure out what. Not yet."

I rubbed my arms, suddenly chilled. The hits just didn't stop coming. "I don't like this."

"Neither do I."

"Are we safe to stay here?"

"Like I said, I haven't found anything. But I'll definitely be keeping my eyes open."

"I just want this to be over, Chase," I muttered.

He pulled me toward him. "I know. Me too."

A knock sounded at the door. Chase grabbed his gun before stomping that way. But when he pulled it open, Ralph and Olivia stood there.

Their eyes widened when they saw Chase's gun. He quickly lowered it and muttered an apology.

"I guess everyone is on edge," Olivia said with a frown.

"You could say that," Chase said.

"We brought sandwiches." Ralph held up a bag from our favorite sandwich place. "Actually, it was Olivia's idea. She's the more thoughtful one."

"That's nice of you," Chase said.

"Why don't we sit down? Both of you look like you could use some food." Ralph walked toward the kitchen.

I lingered behind and gave Olivia a hug. "Thanks for coming."

"How are you doing?" Olivia's concerned eyes studied mine.

I shrugged. "It's been rough."

"I hope they can find whoever's behind this soon."

"Me too."

We sat at the table and pulled out turkey and roast beef sandwiches. I longed for regular conversation, but I knew that wouldn't happen. There was too much at stake here.

"So, strangest thing," Ralph started. "I tried to get in touch with my friend who was being extorted."

I took a bite of my sandwich, unsure that I wanted to know where this was going.

"I haven't been able to get hold of him for several days, so I started thinking the worst," Ralph continued. "But I stopped by his condo today."

"And?" I wiped my mouth, sensing he was going to say something important.

"It turns out he was in a car accident."

Chase's gaze met mine as we both connected the puzzle piece at the same time.

"Wait, was your friend Tyler Billings?" I asked.

Ralph pushed his eyebrows together, not bothering to hide his confusion. "It was. How did you know that? I was careful not to mention his name."

"Because Tyler Billings is connected with the case I'm working on now," Chase said. "I'm going to need you to tell me more."

———

THROUGH TALKING TO RALPH, we discovered that Tyler Billings had cheated on his now-estranged wife. He was in the middle of divorce proceedings, and someone had threatened to send compromising, date-stamped photos to his wife's lawyer if Tyler didn't pay up.

Ralph didn't condone Tyler's actions, but he'd turned to Chase for advice since he was being blackmailed.

Tyler had decided not to pay.

Four days later, he was in the hospital after his car's brakes mysteriously stopped working. Police had originally assumed it had been a mechanical issue. In the meantime, Tyler was still sedated and unable to speak.

The same pattern was emerging, one that involved blackmail.

All the cases seemed connected.

The question was why? And had I really been pulled into this because I'd been investigating Hayden's death? Had someone wanted to silence me that badly—and to play his twisted game in the process?

It was the only thing that made sense.

But now the bigger question was, who was this Gerald Moven guy? Who was he *really*?

Felix had done a background check on him, as well as on Perry Gutherson. Neither of them appeared to be real. The identities were fabricated.

The real person behind this was using multiple identities in order to send the police on a wild goose chase.

Chase leaned back into the couch after Ralph and Olivia left. He was processing. I'd seen it before. He needed time to let his thoughts cycle.

"There's something that's bugging me," he finally said. "So this guy discovers you're investigating Axon and getting too close to answers. He gets nervous and starts to plan how he can take you down. But how did he discover that you liked all things retro?"

"I have no idea." I'd thought about it myself. There was so much I still didn't know. "This guy knows when I'm at the police station. Knows when I'm at home.

Knows when I'm here. Normally, I'd say he must be tracking my phone. But I don't even have my phone. So how?"

"What if it's someone who knows you?" Chase asked.

"I guess that's a possibility, though it's not one I want to think about. I mean, who would it be? Not my family. Jamie is really my closest friend, and I know she's not behind this."

"You're right. It doesn't make a lot of sense. But somehow this guy is getting information. He may be a genius when it comes to technology, but some of these things go beyond technology, you know? Like how did he know this Perry guy went into your office? Somehow, he knew that, and he decided to use the man's name. And how did he know that your brother knew Tyler? Did he target Kurt Casey first and then decide to pull him into your abduction?"

"Those are a lot of good questions." I suddenly sat up, an idea hitting me. "Can I see your laptop?"

Chase handed it to me.

I typed in a few things until a YouTube video popped up. It was one Sarah had made for an assignment at school. I pressed play and showed Chase the screen.

"Holly loves things from times past," Sarah narrated. On the screen was a picture of me in one of my A-line dresses, holding some homemade cookies and offering a little curtsey to the camera. "She likes to cook and clean and make people feel at home. Some people would call her old-fashioned because she loves life in the 50s. I just think she's cool."

"What is this?" Chase asked.

"Sarah had to do a project for school—a video of someone she admired. She picked me."

"Well, I know you're honored. And you could be right. If someone came across this, it could have given them the ammunition they needed to set up this whole scenario."

"Maybe it was then a matter of putting things in place. Maybe this guy saw the article on Kurt Casey and knew his retro home would work perfectly for the scheme he was developing. He did his homework first, found some dirt on Kurt, and decided to pull him into this plan."

"And Perry?"

"What if the real bad guy somehow found out Perry visited Ralph's office and talked to me?" I continued. "He could have planted Perry's picture on the old Axon website just to throw us off."

"And Tyler?"

I nibbled on my bottom lip for a minute. "Tyler was in the accident four days ago, right?"

"That's correct."

"So . . . maybe this guy needed another scapegoat. Could he have been monitoring your calls? Ralph's?"

"My line is secure. To listen in on my phone calls . . . it would be impressive."

"So it's unlikely but not out of the question?"

"I suppose."

At that moment, Chase's cell phone rang. He excused himself and went to answer in the other room. When he came back, a deep frown was on his face.

"What is it?" I asked.

"Out of curiosity, earlier I called the motel where Kari had been staying," Chase said. "We had a bust there a few months ago."

"A bust?"

"This guy was filming things in hotel rooms—unbeknownst to the person inside."

"That's horrible."

"I know. I sent a guy out to check the room where Kari was staying, just to make sure that this guy wasn't up to his old tricks again. We arrested the ringleader, but he had other little minions at his disposal."

"And?"

"And my guy found a camera just like the one this perp was using."

I sat up straight. "Really? Where is it?"

"He's bringing it over."

"You're not giving it to Wilson?"

Chase frowned. "I would . . . but the truth is that whoever this inside guy is . . . I'm afraid he might have a connection to the police department."

CHAPTER TWENTY-THREE

"REALLY?" I nearly squealed, my voice rising just above a fever pitch. "You think this guy could be a cop?"

Chase leaned forward, resting his elbows on his legs as he stared in the distance with a steely focus. "Maybe not a cop. But someone who works with cops. I don't know. It makes the most sense that this person would have seen you at the station. Would know what we're planning before we even execute the ideas."

I shook my head. "I think you made the right call by asking this guy to bring the video here. You don't want the wrong person to get their hands on it. Is this someone you can definitely trust?"

"Yes, he's someone I've worked with for the past four years."

Fifteen minutes later, the officer brought the camera

to Chase. It was small, and I wasn't sure how he planned on watching whatever was on it.

But, with more skill than I knew Chase had, he pulled out a little disk and managed to insert it into his computer. Images filled the screen. We skipped over most of them until we reached the moment Kari arrived.

I watched her in the hotel room, feeling a little guilty at the invasion of her privacy. But she almost looked normal as she lay on the bed watching TV and staring at her fingernails.

Finally, we reached the moment where she perked up in bed. She looked at the door as if someone had knocked. I held my breath.

Was this it? The moment we'd find out the truth?

I leaned closer to the computer screen, waiting to see who came inside.

A man wearing a black hoodie appeared at the corner of the screen.

I squinted, hoping that he would turn toward the camera so we could see his face.

The man may have been a tech genius, but he obviously hadn't had a clue another criminal had already left a camera in this room. For the first time, crime was paying off.

I watched, still holding my breath.

Finally, the man glanced back.

I sucked in a deep breath, uncertain if I'd seen correctly.

Because that had looked like . . .

"Felix," Chase muttered. "That was Felix."

———

EVERYTHING THAT HAPPENED NEXT SEEMED like a blur.

Chase called a friend with the state police who told him Felix no longer worked for them. Our Felix also didn't match the description of the true Felix, who'd moved to California and taken a security job out there. The pretend Felix's picture was now being run through databases in hopes of getting a match.

So far, this guy had pretended to be numerous people. He'd taken their names. Their photos. Their identities. But what was his real name?

Chase had been on the phone ever since his discovery. He'd put in a call to Wilson, who'd said Felix had gone back to his hotel for the evening.

A squad car had been sent to the hotel, but there was no Felix.

Now it was a waiting game.

As weariness pressed in on me, I stayed awake, determined to hear any news as soon as it became available. Chase seemed just as anxious for an update. We sat on the couch, making phone calls, searching for things on the laptop, and waiting.

I'd made some popcorn, and we drank some sweet

tea, more to pass time than from hunger. As I popped a buttery kernel into my mouth, my thoughts circled.

"Tell me about Hugo," I finally said. I knew the question didn't seem connected to what was currently taking place, but I still had some uncertainties.

Chase flinched before setting his tea down and leaning back. "I don't know what there is to tell. I never found him. I only know that his name was thrown when I was following a lead. I've been looking for him since then."

"No other evidence has popped up?"

"No." Chase sagged against the couch, looking exhausted. "When my brother was shot, I figured his death was a result of his involvement in the drug culture. I assumed Hugo was associated with that."

"Was he?"

"Hayden was deeper involved in the drug culture than I wanted to admit. He liked nice things, but he needed money to afford them. Drugs—and dealing them—seemed to offer him some of those opportunities. That also meant he got involved with some dangerous people."

"That's not good."

"I was able to question some people in the park where he was shot. Everyone assumed he was killed in a mugging. But I knew there was more to it than that."

"Do you have any theories about this Hugo guy, now that you've had time to think about it?"

"I've often wondered if he was a hired gun," Chase said. "Only a professional could disappear that easily."

I turned toward Chase, desperate to understand him. "I just can't comprehend why you blame yourself."

The same heaviness came over Chase again. He only talked about his brother in snippets. I could tell it was hard for him. Part of me didn't want to bring it up, but the other part of me had to know.

There were too many connections for me to not have all the facts.

Chase let out a sigh. "I saw my brother going places he shouldn't have gone and getting involved with things that he shouldn't. I tried to warn him to stay away from that lifestyle. I knew it was nothing but trouble."

"But he didn't stay away?"

Chase ran a hand over his face and his voice sobered even more. "He didn't. I actually gave him an ultimatum. I told him if he didn't walk away that I would." His voice caught.

I waited for him to gather his thoughts and finish.

"Long story short, I walked away. I thought that would jog some sense into him, but it didn't. He continued doing what he was doing. I was watching, waiting for an opportunity to arrest him. I thought maybe jailtime would open his eyes. But I never caught him."

"I see."

Chase turned toward me, his eyes locking with mine. "The thing is, Holly, if I hadn't been so stubborn, if I hadn't given him that ultimatum, if I'd been there for him . . . maybe none of this would have happened."

I reached for his arm and squeezed it. More than anything, I wanted to take away his pain. Easier said than done, however. "You can't know that."

He shrugged. "I can't. But that's what haunts me every night. That's what's been so hard to get past. I was his brother. I should have been there for him. I should have protected him. But I didn't."

"Chase—"

He turned toward me, taking my hand into his. "And that's what worries me about you. I want to be there for you. I don't want to give you ultimatums. But I still fear I won't be able to protect you like I should."

I traced Chase's face with my fingers, wishing I could soothe the lines of worry there. "If anything happens to me, it won't be your fault. You have to know that."

"But I'm afraid I won't."

My heart pounded so hard in my chest that it almost hurt. He meant those words. He would always blame himself if anything happened to the people he loved, and no one would change his mind.

His phone rang, pulling us from the tension in the room. He spoke into it a few minutes before turning toward me.

"They got a match on Felix's picture," he said. "I think we might finally know his real name."

CHAPTER TWENTY-FOUR

CHASE and I headed down the road. Not only did we have a name, but we also had an address. Though it was late and night had fallen hours ago, Chase wanted to be there and see for himself as this man was arrested.

"Who is he?" I asked, unable to wait any longer. Would his real name sound familiar? Would this be the missing piece that pulled everything together and gave us the answers we needed?

"His real name is Lars Dahlman." Chase stared straight ahead, his gaze set and determined.

"Dahlman?" I repeated, uncertain if I'd heard correctly.

"This guy definitely delights in the absurd. He probably made a play on his name when he chose his costume, almost so he could silently mock us."

I had no doubt that Chase was correct. And the name didn't ring any bells. "So who is Lars Dahlman?"

"From what Wilson told me, he's actually Scandinavian, from Norway. He came to the States about ten years ago. He's a renowned hacker with a large bank account."

"So is this Lars guy the one who started Axon? Or is this all another smokescreen?"

"That's a great question. I feel like this is the real guy, not another red herring. We're sending some pictures of this guy—with all of his various identities—over to Mitch to see if he recognizes him. We've had the wool pulled over our eyes so many times, we need to verify things."

I shifted in my seat, trying to keep my excitement at bay. We still had a lot more work to do. Or, I should say, the police still had a lot more work to do. "You never saw this man when your brother worked at the company or when you investigated afterward?"

Chase shook his head. "Dahlman, known to me then as Gerald Moven, was working out of the country—supposedly—when everything went down. I didn't even view him as a suspect."

"Convenient that he had such a strong alibi."

"I know. I tried to research him, but there was surprisingly very little online about him, especially considering his work relied on having a social media presence."

"Of course, we don't know what's reality. He was probably online using aliases and fake photos."

"You're probably right."

I leaned back. "So, since you know his real name, what's his real story? Do you know?"

"Read for yourself what Wilson just sent." He handed me his phone, and I stared at the screen.

"According to what I'm reading, his background seems fairly normal," I said. "His parents have been married for more than thirty years. He has a younger sister. He hacked into a government website and released some sensitive emails that made several Norwegian leaders look like fools. He fled the country before being caught. Some of his friends called him a practical joker."

"That all seems to fit."

"How did he pretend to be a cop like he did?" I asked. "He tricked everyone in the office. That's no small task."

"He had the right name, the right badge, the right know-how. He integrated so easily that no one really questioned him."

Though a profile was beginning to come together in my mind, there was still one thing that bothered me. "Chase, I still don't understand why he targeted us . . ."

"Maybe we'll find out some answers soon." Chase pulled to a stop in front of a decent-sized house in an upper-middle-class neighborhood. Police cars bordered the residences, and neighbors had come out to stare as the SWAT team surrounded the place.

Chase and I climbed out and took our place near the police line.

Chase shook his head as he stared at the scene in front of us. "This guy was sitting right in front of us, and no one recognized him. I can only imagine the pleasure he got from that fact."

"Do you think he's inside?" I nodded toward the house.

"We can only hope."

"But he's always been two steps ahead . . ." My thoughts churned inside me as I pieced together what I knew about this man. One thought kept trying to take center stage.

"What are you thinking, Holly?"

A bad feeling snaked up my spine. Was I reading too much into this? Was I paranoid?

Maybe.

But what if I wasn't?

"Chase . . . how do we know this guy hasn't been somehow listening to all the communication between police right now?"

"I suppose we don't know that."

"So he could know that your guys were coming?"

Chase's face went pale, and he took a step forward. "Get behind the car. Now!"

I hurried across the sidewalk toward Chase's car.

Once I was safely behind it, I watched as Chase rushed beyond the police line.

He began a heated conversation with Wilson, just as the SWAT team entered the house.

My stomach twisted as I waited.

I hoped I was wrong. I really hoped I was.

But just as the thought entered my mind, an explosion rocked the neighborhood. Debris rained through the air in daggers of fire.

I ducked behind the car, but my gaze stayed on Chase.

He was okay. Wilson was okay.

But this whole thing had been a trap.

———

THREE MEN HAD BEEN INJURED when they'd entered Dahlman's house. They were at the hospital, still hanging on. I prayed for good news. I could only imagine what their loved ones were experiencing.

As I'd feared, Dahlman had known they were coming, and he'd planned this. The question was, where was he now? Where was Kari? They hadn't found her body inside. Not yet, at least.

No one knew that answer. No one knew how Dahlman had been able to get past police security checkpoints and fool law enforcement. But he had.

Chase and I had eventually gone back to his place.

I'd gone to bed, unable to stay awake any longer.

But Chase had remained awake, on the phone and on his laptop, trying to track down leads. By morning, I hoped he'd find something.

"We've set up false leads," was the first thing Chase said to me when I emerged from my bedroom at six a.m. "We've set up a whole chain of correspondence to make it sound like we're going to do a raid of one of the locations Dahlman frequents. Meanwhile, we have a new tech guy who's come in, and he's going to trace this guy. It's a complicated process, but he thinks he'll be able to ping his location."

"That sounds like the perfect plan." I sat beside him at the kitchen table, anxious to hear more. "But what do we do until then?"

"We wait."

I hated waiting. I hated not being in on the action.

For the next two hours, I made cookies. I cleaned. I felt more like myself. But I still refused to wear my dresses. I wasn't ready for that yet. I needed to separate my way of dressing from the crime committed against me.

But I wanted to do whatever I could to keep my mind occupied.

Finally, the call from Wilson came just after lunchtime. Chase put the phone on speaker.

"We got him," Wilson told Chase. "The plan worked. Dahlman was listening to us from a building where he'd been renting an office—under an alternative identity, of course. Lars Dahlman is now in official police custody."

"Is he talking?" Chase asked.

"No, not yet. He said he'll only talk to you and Holly."

"Me and Holly?" Chase jerked his gaze toward me and shook his head. "Having Holly face this guy is out of the question."

"I agree that it's not a good idea." Wilson let out a sigh and seemed to move on. "We also found Kari Leblanc at the office complex where he was hiding out."

"Was she okay?" Chase asked.

"She appeared to be fine. We have her in custody at the station now."

Everything in me wanted to go down to the station and help figure out what was happening. But this was one area that I couldn't insert myself into without an invitation. That invitation had to be from Wilson or Chase, not from Dahlman.

"He really said he'll talk only to Holly and me?" Chase finally said.

"That's correct. The two of you together."

Chase let out a long breath and glanced at me. I nodded to let him know that I was okay with it. Finally, he frowned and raised the phone back to his mouth.

"We'll be there in a half an hour," he said. "But, if at any point I feel like things are going south, Holly is out."

"I would expect nothing less."

Dread and excitement collided inside me. I was going. Maybe I would get answers.

But doubt also clouded my thoughts.

That had seemed easy. Almost too easy, hadn't it? Or had we really outsmarted this man?

CHAPTER TWENTY-FIVE

I FIDGETED as I prepared myself to talk to Lars Dahlman. Though I wanted to talk to him, I couldn't deny that facing the man who'd abducted me sent shivers down my spine.

"You don't have to do this." Chase paused outside the door to the interrogation room and looked me straight in the eye.

"I know. I want to. I want answers."

He stared at me another moment before nodding. "If at any time you want out, you just let me know. There's no pressure on my end for you to be in there."

"I appreciate that, Chase."

I wiped my sweaty palms on my jeans. Yes, my jeans. There was no way I wanted this man to get any satisfaction by seeing me in a dress. I still got a sickly feeling in my stomach when I thought about that house he'd trapped me in.

Together, we stepped into the room. My stomach turned as Dahlman came into view.

He looked so smug as he sat there . . . which again made me pause. Something just didn't feel right about all of this.

"So you figured it out." Dahlman smirked.

He didn't have dark hair as I'd expected. He must have been wearing a wig when he posed as Felix. At the moment, he looked so normal with his square face and light-colored hair. He wasn't sweaty or disheveled. No, he could very well be doing a job interview right now.

And he had an accent. A Norwegian accent. He'd masterfully sounded All American when I'd heard him talk before, both as my abductor and as Felix.

"It took you long enough," Dahlman crooned, lounging back in his chair.

Chase scowled as he took a seat across from him. "You think you're the smartest man in the room, don't you?"

"I think I am?" Dahlman's eyebrows shot up. "I am the smartest man."

"But you were caught."

His smile dimmed—but only a little. "You all got lucky."

I may have let out a little snort.

Dahlman's gaze traveled to me. "Good to see you again, Holly. I was quite sad that our time together was cut short. Your chicken pot pie smelled exquisite."

Queasiness rose in me, which I was sure was his desired effect. "You're sick."

"I prefer to say brilliant."

Chase squeezed my knee beneath the table before opening a folder he had brought with him. "So, you ran the Axon Corporation. You knew my brother."

Dahlman smiled again. "That's correct. I was so sorry to hear about his passing."

"Why didn't you just kill me?" I blurted. I knew I probably shouldn't interrupt, but the question burned in my mind. Asking it was the only way to relieve the sear of the flames, to find any relief.

Dahlman leaned closer. "Because sometimes there are better things to do than kill. Sometimes, it's better to watch your target slowly die inside."

His words turned my stomach. He was sick and twisted. And suddenly, I just wanted to be away from him. But first I wanted to hear him out.

"Why have all of these casualties if Chase and I were the target?"

He grinned again. "Because that's what makes it fun. I figure out what I need to do. I put a plan in place to accomplish it. And I always say it's better to kill two birds with one stone, if possible. So I looked at the people who could help me, I found the cracks in their lives, exploited them, and it was truly a win-win —for me."

People were just pawns in his game.

Kurt Casey's death meant nothing to him, nor did Barbara's. Definitely not Hayden's.

And I was sure if I had died, that would also mean nothing to him—not as long as he got what he wanted.

This man was a psychopath. Thank God, he'd been caught.

Now I just prayed that this was truly over.

———

CHASE and I met in the hallway an hour later, after we'd finished talking to Dahlman. I thought I'd feel better. Instead, I still felt uneasy, and I couldn't shake the feeling.

"It seems like a slam dunk, Holly." He paused in front of me and lowered his voice as we stood in the dim space. "He's pretty much owned up to everything."

"That's great." I heard the uncertainty in my own voice, though I willed it not to be there.

Chase twisted his head. "Why don't you sound happy?"

I shrugged, wondering how much to say. "I don't know. Something just feels off. Am I the only one who senses it?"

"I'm not sure what could be off. Everything seems to be lining up. Maybe it will just take a while for it to sink in that the guy who did this to you has finally been arrested."

I nodded, realizing the truth of his words. "You're probably right. I'm just overthinking things."

He squeezed my arm. "This should all be over, Holly. All of it. We have reason to celebrate."

I tried to smile, but my lips didn't cooperate. "I know. That's amazing, isn't it?"

"It is. Now, do you want to talk to Kari?"

"I'd love to."

"Good. Maybe she has some of those final answers we've been looking for."

I could only hope.

But as we stepped toward a different interrogation room, another memory begged for my attention. I paused, but only for a minute, as a flashback hit me.

I was back at the house. My captor had stepped inside. I was about to serve him dinner. He put his hand on my waist.

As he did, I heard another sound.

My heart thrummed in my ears as I tried to remember, to erase any doubts.

It was the sound of the camera moving, wasn't it?

Had someone else been watching the whole exchange?

I didn't know. I wasn't sure that I hadn't imagined it all.

But I didn't like the bad feeling that had returned to my gut.

CHAPTER TWENTY-SIX

I STARED at Kari across the table. I'd decided to keep my realization to myself—for now. I needed to know if I was making up things out of the fear I'd missed something or if it had been an honest memory. I still wasn't sure.

Instead, I focused my attention on Kari. She looked better now than she had when I'd last seen her. She appeared to have showered. Her hair was clean. Her skin no longer had smudges of grime. The flannel shirt and jeans she wore appeared to be new.

Chase sat beside me, but he didn't say anything. He waited for me to start instead.

"Has anything you've told me been the truth?" My throat burned as the question left my lips.

Her chin trembled. "Yes, what I told you last time

was true. My dad was the biological half-brother of your father, and that's how I managed to track you down."

"Were you involved with Lars Dahlman?" Chase asked.

"No!" Her face fell. "I mean, yes. Kind of. It's confusing."

"What does that mean?" Chase said. "What's so confusing about it?"

Kari let out a long sigh and leaned back in her chair. "I mean, this guy approached me a couple of weeks ago. He had a police badge and told me he needed my help."

"You believed him?" I asked. She didn't strike me as the naïve type.

"He seemed legitimate. There was nothing about him that raised any red flags."

Chase leaned back and crossed his legs, as if settling in to hear a long story. "What happened next?"

"He told me he would be in touch when the time was right, but that it involved some crimes that had been going on in the Queensgate area. He told me that there could be some corrupt officers, so I shouldn't mention this to anyone. He said he was with Internal Affairs."

We waited as Kari seemed to compose herself. Either she was a great actress or this had really shaken her up. Her motions were jerky. Her voice trembled. Her gaze skittered around the room.

"He showed up at the motel that morning and said

he needed to get me out of there before anyone else arrived. He took me back to his office and told me I had to stay there until he knew I'd be safe."

"What about the blood on the floor of the motel room?" Chase asked. "How did that get there?"

That was a great question. I'd almost forgotten about that.

"He had a bag of blood. I don't know where it was from or what kind it was. He said he needed to make it look like I'd been snatched. Said otherwise, I'd look guilty."

I had to practice the suspension of my disbelief as I listened to her story. I wasn't sure I bought it.

"So he took you back to the house. What then?" Chase continued. "Did you ask him any questions about the nature of his investigation?"

"I wanted to, but I just tried to keep my mouth shut." Kari's chin trembled. "My mouth always gets me in trouble, and I decided to change that. I didn't want to make a mess of things this time."

Of course. This was the one time she'd decided to behave. Still, she might only be alive right now because of that, so I couldn't complain.

"What happened next?" Chase asked. "What did he say he wanted you to do?"

She drew in another shaky breath. "He said I was going to be framed for this crime, the one where Holly was abducted. He was trying to make sure I stayed safe.

He said some corrupt cops were going to make things dicey for a while and that he might eventually need my help. The next thing I knew, the police barged in, and we were both arrested."

I wanted to believe her. I really did. But Kari lied effortlessly. Who was to say she wasn't doing that now?

Her story was big. Outlandish. Slightly unbelievable. But that didn't mean it wasn't true.

I glanced at Chase, trying to tell if he bought what she tried to sell. I couldn't read his expression. I could only see that he was being cautious.

"What are you going to do with me now?" Kari's eyes were wide with fear as she stared at Chase.

"That's for Detective Wilson to decide," Chase said. "He's heading up this case."

"Will I go to jail?"

"I guess that depends on whether or not your story checks out." Chase stood and glanced at me. "Come on, let's get out of here. We have other work to do."

"Wait!" Kari called.

We froze and turned back to her.

She let out a long breath. "I don't know if it's important or not, but this guy was talking on the phone to someone else. Talking a lot."

"You think he was working with someone?" Chase asked.

Kari shrugged. "I have no idea. At the time, I thought he was talking to his contacts with Internal

Affairs. But now that I know the truth . . . he could have been talking to anyone."

I needed to tell Chase about my memory, I decided. Even if I was wrong . . . he needed to know.

But before I could share, his phone buzzed. He punched a couple things on his screen and frowned. He held up his phone for me to see.

A video played there

A video of Drew. My ex, Drew.

He sat on a couch in a retro-style living room holding his head as if it hurt.

All the air rushed out of my lungs.

Someone had abducted Drew, I realized.

My instincts had been right. Lars Dahlman was working with someone.

This wasn't over yet. Far from it.

———

I PACED the hall of the police station while Chase questioned Dahlman again. Another crew had been sent back to the house where I'd been found to see if Drew was there. I knew he wouldn't be. It didn't fit into this game that had been so carefully planned.

Drew? Why in the world had Drew been involved with this? It didn't make sense.

I paced still, feeling like I was beside myself.

What were we missing? Who in the world could

Dahlman be working with? Would he really give up that information?

I couldn't make sense of things, but I desperately wanted to.

Please let Drew be okay. I kept praying the prayer over and over again. The thought of something happening to him . . . it crushed my spirit.

He was innocent in all of this. I was the one who stuck my nose into other people's business. I usually got myself in trouble.

But not Drew. He was a good guy.

I glanced at the time on my phone. How long was Chase going to talk to Dahlman? What had they found at that house?

Not knowing was killing me.

As much as I wanted to believe they'd rescued Drew and everything would be okay, I knew better.

Dahlman and his accomplice were playing a twisted game, one in which they were always the champions.

Finally, Chase stepped out of the interrogation room, a stormy expression on his face.

"What did you find out?" I rushed.

"That man is as smug as they come," Chase seethed. "He seems to be enjoying this."

"Did he tell you where Drew is?"

"No, of course he didn't. He said he doesn't know." Chase held out his phone. "But we just got another video."

I looked at the screen. Drew sat on the couch, a dazed expression on his face still. Then he held up a sign to the camera.

My life will be spared in return for the lives of Chase and Holly.

I sucked in a breath. What?

He picked up another sign.

Wait for further instructions.

Drew looked at the camera, still holding the signs. At once, he broke character and yelled, "Don't do it, Holly!"

Then the screen went black.

CHAPTER TWENTY-SEVEN

"THERE'S no way you're going." Chase sliced his hand through the air.

"He'll kill Drew if I don't."

"If you do go, they'll kill you too." Anger came in waves off Chase as he paced the conference room. Other detectives, including Wilson, were in the room, along with the police captain. They all tried to figure out the best plan of action.

The house where I'd been kept had been checked and found empty. We didn't know where Drew was being held, and as quickly as the IT guys tried to trace the source of the message, everyone in the room knew it would do no good.

Dahlman and whomever he was working with . . . they were tech geniuses. They knew how to reroute signals and maximize their capabilities for the ultimate confusion.

And that left us at their mercy.

"I want to go," I repeated. "I can't let something happen to Drew. He has nothing to do with this."

"Neither do you." Chase's nostrils flared as his emotions ran high. "You can't go."

I didn't blame him for his strong feelings. But there were other issues at play here. "Chase . . ."

"Wait." Wilson stood from his seat at the table. "This might be the only way we can get to this guy."

"It's a horrible idea." Chase still stomped back and forth.

"It's the only idea that would work," Wilson said. "We can protect you both."

"We can put gear on you," Captain Myers said. "Tracers. Microphones."

"This person will figure it out." Chase stubbornly shook his head.

Captain Myers raised his head, his gaze zeroing in on Chase. "Then what do you suggest?"

"I don't suggest anything."

I stepped forward, knowing my opinion meant nothing. Still, I needed to speak. "All I know is that we have to move quickly. We don't know how much time we have."

"We can't be hasty. We need to figure out who he's working with." Chase raised his hands into the air.

"Who have we missed? It's not Kari. We have her in custody. Have we searched this guy's bank records? Talked to neighbors to see who he's been hanging out with? Have we searched to see who else is left over from Axon that he might be working with?"

"We're covering all of those angles," Wilson said. "Answers are slowly coming in."

"Have you found out anything?" Chase asked.

"No, not really. There was one man who came over to Dahlman's place a few times, and a woman who showed up on occasion, according to neighbors. It doesn't give us much to go on."

"We can't check his social media, because we can't trust anything we find online. It's hard to know what to believe, for that matter." Chase's entire body looked tight as he said the words. This was all getting to him.

He'd thought it was over.

But maybe it was just starting.

"We have another video," Wilson announced, sitting up in his seat and holding up his phone. "This one was sent to the department."

Everyone gathered around to see it.

It was Drew. On the couch he held up another sign.

You have one hour to get here. Instructions will be texted to Chase. Follow them exactly.

On the side of the screen, an arm stretched forward holding a gun that was aimed at his head.

————

TWENTY MINUTES LATER, Chase and I were on the road. He still wasn't happy, and I couldn't blame him.

Truth be told, I wasn't happy either. But what choice did I have? I couldn't let Drew suffer and die.

The good news was that I had a bullet-proof vest on beneath my shirt, as did Chase. My earrings contained trackers. A microphone had been attached beneath Chase's shirt. The police should be monitoring everything we were doing.

There were several cars following us. Others meeting us there. But we couldn't let the fact that they were there be known.

Everything was risky. Then, again, so was life.

"I don't like this," Chase muttered as we pulled into the neighborhood in his car. The same neighborhood where I'd been abducted but a different house. Officers had checked many of these homes, but they hadn't been able to get into them all. They hadn't had enough time.

"I don't either," I told him, trying to hide my anxiety.

"If anything happens to you . . ." His voice caught and he touched his neck, his entire body looking tense.

"You'll be there to protect me."

He glanced at me. The heaviness in his gaze made it clear how much pressure he felt. "But what if I can't?"

"Even if you can't, it will be okay. I'd rather die doing the right thing than to live with myself knowing I could have done better." I didn't say the words lightly, but I meant them with all my being.

His fingers skimmed across my face before tangling in my hair. "You're one in a million, Holly."

"I think you're pretty great too."

"If we don't get out of this—"

My throat tightened. "Don't talk like that."

"No, I want to say this. If we don't get out of this, I want you to know that you're the best thing that ever happened to me. You've made my life better and complete. Thank you."

"Oh, Chase . . ." My heart squeezed with emotion as I stared at his face. At his tousled blond hair. The depths of his blue eyes. The perfect lines of his jaw. They were perfect to me, at least. "I love you."

"I love you too." He quickly kissed me before glancing at the house in the distance. "You're absolutely sure you want to do this?"

I nodded. "Yeah, I am."

He turned the car off and stepped out. He took my hand as we walked toward the front door. I had no idea what we were going to face inside. I had no idea if I would make it out alive.

But I knew I was doing the right thing, despite the tremble of fear that started down deep inside me.

CHAPTER TWENTY-EIGHT

WE STEPPED INTO THE HOUSE. The front door was unlocked, just like we'd been told.

I glanced around, hardly able to breathe. This house appeared to have the same layout as the one I'd been held captive in. To my right, there was a dining room. Farther down, on the left, was the hallway leading to the bedrooms. Straight ahead we'd run into the kitchen and living room.

Unlike the last house, this one wasn't decorated. There was no furniture or anything on the walls. Wood floors were beneath our feet, and the walls had been painted a calming gray.

It was also suspiciously quiet inside.

"Hello?" Chase called.

No one answered.

He pushed himself in front of me and crept forward. Forward. Forward.

I expected a jump scare. A figure to appear from the shadows. I halfway even expected another bomb. But there was nothing.

Finally, we paused in an empty kitchen.

There was no sign of Drew, and no sign that he'd ever been here even.

A shudder raked through me. Had this been a trap? A distraction? I had no idea.

"There's a note." Chase strode across the room and picked up a paper from the kitchen counter. "It says we're to go out the back door and into the house behind this one."

"Chase—" Panic raced through me. This wasn't part of the plan.

He turned toward me and said, "We've got this, Holly."

I swallowed hard, wishing I felt as certain. It didn't matter. What choice did we have but to obey? Especially when I remembered the look in Drew's eyes in that video.

Besides, the police were tracking us.

With trepidation, we stepped out the back door. I glanced around. From where we stood now, I doubted anyone could see us. I certainly couldn't see them. The house perfectly concealed us.

We had to be careful what we said also because we

had no idea what was being monitored by the person behind this ordeal. Cameras and microphones could be set up, for all we knew. We couldn't risk giving anything away.

Slowly, we walked across the lawn to the house located directly behind it. As we reached the back door, I glanced behind me one more time.

I still couldn't see the front yard. Couldn't get a glimpse of anyone who might be monitoring us.

That was exactly what this person wanted, wasn't it?

He'd suspected people would be watching us, and he'd had a backup plan. He'd thought of everything.

My stomach churned at the thought of it.

Chase and I stepped through the unlocked back door of the house and into the living room. I knew that, just as in the other homes, there were built-ins on two walls. Exquisite craftsmanship adorned the crown molding and the columns that separated this space from the kitchen.

But I hardly looked at those things now. I hardly noticed the two blue couches there. The woven rug resting on the floor.

All I could see was Drew sitting in front of us. His hands and feet were bound, and a gag stretched over his mouth.

I sucked in a deep breath, wanting to rush toward him and help.

But I knew that would be too easy. We had to proceed with caution.

As soon as the door closed behind us, someone stepped out, gun in hand.

But it wasn't a man.

It was a woman wearing a doll mask with a sickly plastic grin.

A woman?

What?

Just who else was involved with this?

———

"YOU TWO, SIT." The woman pointed her gun at the second couch, one that was set up at a right angle to the one where Drew sat.

Chase raised his hands and kept his voice placid as he said, "We're going. Don't do anything drastic."

"I'll judge what's drastic." Her growling voice contradicted her smiling mask and made everything feel even more disturbing.

Chase and I sat on the couch, just as we were told. My feet nudged the rug in front of me, and I wanted nothing more than to put a nonslip pad beneath it.

Really, Holly? That's what you think about right now?

I knew the thought was just a result of the anxiety that gripped me.

I glanced at Drew. His eyes were wide. His skin was pale. Blood trickled from a scrape at his temple.

But, overall, he looked okay. I prayed he would stay that way. *Please, Lord.*

"You have no idea who I am, do you?" The woman strode in front of us, her brown eyes barely visible because of the mask.

"Should we know?" My voice came out as a croak as I stared up at her.

She let out a laugh, the gun still firmly in her hands. "No, I suppose you wouldn't. Detective Dexter should, though. Then again, all he's been concerned about for all these years is his brother."

Chase's gaze nearly burned into hers. "Did you know my brother?"

"As a matter of fact, I did. I worked with Hayden at Axon." Though we couldn't see her face, I could hear the pleasure in her voice. It rang out loud and clear.

Chase sucked in a quick breath but still remained calm. "Did you?"

"Something else you probably don't know is this— it's your fault my boyfriend is dead. You set all of this in motion when you didn't mind your own business. And then your little girlfriend started digging into my company. The two of you are nothing but trouble. But I'm going to take care of that."

Chase stared at her, a knot of confusion between his eyebrows. "Who was your boyfriend?"

"Hugo Miller."

"Hugo was your boyfriend?" Chase repeated, disbelief stretching through his voice.

I didn't think either of us had seen that one coming.

But, suddenly, things made more sense. If this woman in some way attributed Hugo's death to Chase, then she had a personal reason to hate Chase, to have a vendetta against him. In her mind, Chase had killed the man she'd loved. Now, she wanted to torture me in return, because, apparently, she thought Chase loved me.

Now, I knew he did. But when all of this had started, we weren't dating.

The thing was . . . Chase had never met Hugo, had he? His name had only come out in a conversation once, from what I recalled.

"Hugo only killed Hayden because I asked him to. But Hayden owed some guys some money—some druggies." She sounded like even saying the word disgusted her. "They thought Hugo might have the money and came after him. Killed him. I had to bury his body myself so the police wouldn't find it."

"Why didn't you want the police to find it?" I asked, still unclear how any of this was Chase's fault.

"If the police discovered Hugo's body, the evidence could lead back to me. I couldn't let that happen."

"I don't understand." Chase remained wedged in front of me, his body tense and on alert. "How is that my fault? I didn't kill Hugo. I didn't even talk to him. Believe me, I wanted to."

"You put out a lead to those guys." Her eyes narrowed with disgust. "About eight months ago, you tracked down one of the dealers Hayden worked with and asked him if he'd heard of a guy named Hugo. They used their connections on the street to track my boyfriend down. They don't easily forget a 300K debt."

"So all of this is about revenge?" Chase bristled as the words left his lips.

"That's right. It's about watching the people we love suffer." She jerked Drew from his seat and put the gun to his head.

Drew let out a moan, and his eyes widened with fear.

My heart pounded in my throat as I watched the scene playing out.

"I'm going to make both of you watch Drew die, and then I'll kill Holly," the woman said. "And you're going to have a front row seat for it all, Chase. So buckle up for the ride."

Sweat sprinkled across my skin. This couldn't be happening. And where was backup? Couldn't they hear what had transpired?

"They won't find you here for a while." She seemed to read my thoughts. "I scrambled the signals and sent them on a bit of a wild goose chase. All your buddies are headed to the other side of the neighborhood now.

They think you walked there and cut through some lawns. Yes, I am a genius. And I did set up some surprises for them when they go inside."

Chase's nostrils flared. "Who are you?"

"You really don't know still?" More satisfaction rang out in the woman's voice. The next instant, she pulled off her mask.

Olivia stood there.

Olivia, the woman my brother was dating. My heart pounded in my ears.

She'd never cared about Ralph, had she? Their relationship was just a scheme to get to me and maybe Chase. She'd been able to keep an eye on this whole situation after I'd escaped.

I had to give both Olivia and Lars kudos. They'd thought everything through. They were brilliant and skilled.

But they were also evil. So, so evil that a knot formed in my chest.

CHAPTER TWENTY-NINE

"WHY WOULD you pull my brother into this?" I asked, my hands clenched at my sides. "And Drew? They have nothing to do with this vendetta you have."

Olivia shrugged. "Because everything feels personal to me. Because you started getting too close to answers, Holly Anna, and I knew I had to stop you. I'd been itching to get some revenge on Chase Dexter for quite a while. Now is the time."

"You're despicable. . ." I muttered.

"I can't tell you how much satisfaction I felt as I watched your face that night at your house as the Doll Man showed up on your TV screen." Olivia flashed a smile. "Watching everything play out was so satisfying."

More anger built up inside me, but Chase nudged

me back down. His touch reminded me to keep my cool. It would go a lot further in this situation than losing it.

Chase turned to Olivia. "You don't have to do this."

"Yes, I do. I have all the money in the world, and you know what? It means nothing without my love by my side. You took that from me, Chase Dexter. You and no one else."

"I'm sorry for your loss," Chase said. "But I didn't do anything to Hugo. I never even saw him."

"Hugo would still be alive right now if you'd just left it alone." Olivia's voice rose. "I didn't even know Hayden had a brother. How does that make you feel? You cared so much about him, but he didn't even bother to mention you."

Chase's cheeks reddened. "We didn't know about each other until a year before Hayden died, but I had hoped that we could get to know each other more. Why did you have him killed?"

Olivia took a step back, but her intense gaze showed she wasn't easing up. She still had her gun—and probably some other tricks up her sleeve. "Hayden had a change of heart. He discovered what we were doing, and we couldn't buy him off. He was going to go to the police. We couldn't let him do that. So we had to set it up to look like a mugging. We had to protect what we were doing."

"What you were doing was blackmailing innocent people and getting their money," Chase said.

"There was nothing innocent about these people," Olivia seethed. "They were doing evil things. Really evil things, and they needed to be exposed."

"But that wasn't your end goal," I muttered, trying to unscramble her supposed motives from the truth. "Your end goal was to get money from them. You can't even make it sound like you were doing this for right-eous reasons."

"They needed to learn their lessons."

"So you started your own business to use as a front. After Axon shut down, you've started other cover orga-nizations—including your current 'grant writing busi-ness.' Correct?" I asked.

How had I not seen it? Olivia had all the traits we'd been looking for in the person who was responsible for this. The way she and Ralph kept showing up together . . . I'd thought it was sweet. Now I knew it was anything but.

And Ralph was going to be heartbroken when he found out the truth.

"That's right," Olivia said. "My brother and I are excellent at developing covers. We haven't been caught until now—and this isn't going to stop us."

"Your brother?" I said. "Lars is your brother?"

Now that she said it, everything made sense.

Olivia smiled again. "We were both blessed with brilliant and devious minds. What can I say? And as you can see, this got personal for me."

She squeezed Drew's arm and rammed the gun into his temple until he groaned. I started to lunge forward, but Chase nudged me back down.

"Now, let's get this taken care of," Olivia growled. "What you don't know is the bigger plan I have here."

"The bigger plan?" I asked. Fear trickled down my spine. This woman's mind . . . I couldn't even fathom what she might be thinking.

Olivia grinned. "That's right. I was able to manipulate some videos, as well as set up some fake information in your bank and email accounts. I'm rather pleased with myself at the final results."

"What did you do, Olivia?" I asked, almost not wanting to know. But I *had* to know.

"I've set everything up to make it look like you and Chase killed Drew before turning on each other. It's really quite wonderful. The video footage is a work of art, if I do say so myself."

"No one will believe that," Chase said.

Olivia flashed a smile. "People will believe anything. All they have to do is see a video online. This will work."

"What about everything that happened up until this?" I asked, buying time. "How will you explain it?"

"The emails will answer it all. They show the two of you scheming this from the start. The love triangle gone bad. It's going to work." She scowled. "Now, let's get this over with."

I STARED at Olivia's gun, unsure what to do.

I felt helpless to stop anything from happening. As much as I wanted to doubt she could have developed a high-quality video that would fool the police, another part of me didn't doubt it at all. This woman knew what she was doing.

She'd known we would arrest Dahlman. She'd used that distraction to abduct Drew. To lure us here.

I was sure she had another plan for getting her brother out of jail.

Olivia appeared to be ready to pull that trigger any time now.

My eyes locked with Drew's. I saw the fear in his gaze.

She was crazy enough to actually do this. I had no doubt about that.

"Olivia, we should talk this through," Chase said.

"There's nothing to talk about. Like I said, the plan has already been set in motion. The world will think you're both evil. Lars and I are going to get away scot-free. That's all there is to it. We'll both become ghosts in the night, and no one will find us."

"What about Kari? How does she tie into all of this?" I asked, still unsure about that aspect.

"We found your relationship with her extremely interesting and knew her involvement would throw you off our trail. So we used that to our advantage. She had nothing to offer us monetarily speaking, but the emotional punch of her possible involvement was satisfying enough."

"Something is wrong with you," I muttered. I couldn't even begin to fathom just what was going through this woman's head.

Olivia's gaze darkened. "Enough talking. I know what you're doing. You think if you talk to me long enough, that your friends will get here and save the day."

I couldn't argue with that.

She stepped back from Drew. "Here goes nothing."

I glanced around, looking for something—anything —that I could use to protect Drew. There were no lamps. No knickknacks. Nothing.

And she was too far away to lunge for her gun. By the time we reached her, she could pull the trigger on Drew and on Chase and me.

There had to be something.

I glanced down, my mind still racing.

"Olivia," Chase started, obviously trying to keep her talking.

The moment of distraction was all I needed.

I reached down and grabbed the rug she stood on. Giving it everything I had, I jerked it.

It slid out from beneath her feet.

She flew into the air, taken off guard. Her gun clattered to the floor.

As she landed on her back, her gaze jerked toward her weapon.

The gun lay on the floor between Olivia and Chase.

I only hoped Chase got to it first.

CHAPTER THIRTY

CHASE DOVE FOR THE GUN. His fingers wrapped around the weapon just seconds before Olivia reached it.

He stood, holding the barrel toward her, and ordered, "Get up."

With her hands raised, Olivia did as he ordered.

Could this really be over? Did I even dare hope that?

Just as the thought entered my mind, the doors burst open. Officers rushed into the room. They cuffed Olivia, despite her grumbling.

As Chase went to oversee her arrest, I hurried to Drew and pulled the gag from his mouth.

"Are you okay?" I asked.

He nodded, still looking pale and shaken. "Yeah, I'm fine."

"I'm so sorry, Drew. I never expected you to get pulled into this."

"It's not your fault, Holly."

I began working the binds at his hands. Chase came over and sliced through them with a pocket knife before I could get the first knot out.

"I'm glad you're okay," he told Drew.

Drew rubbed his wrists, his eyes appeared glazed as he glanced around. "Yeah, me too. Good police work back there. You two do make a good team. And you know what? This kind of life . . . it's not for me."

We all looked back at Olivia as she was being led away. She'd had everything in the world, yet all she'd wanted was more. That selfishness had led to her demise, and I, for one, was happy to see her go to jail for it.

"Who would have thought a rug could save the day?" Chase asked. "That was some fast thinking, Holly."

I shrugged. "My *Good Housekeeping* inclinations are to thank. All I'd been able to think about earlier was how slippery the rug was. Of course, it was still a risk. She could have accidentally pulled the trigger. But I knew I had to do something."

"You did the right thing."

I glanced at Chase. "You know, if what Olivia said was true, then your brother could have easily accepted that money from Axon to pay off his debt to the dealers he was working with. I don't know what was going on in his life when all of this happened, but it sounds like he was trying to do better. To be better."

"That is how it seems, isn't it?"

The paramedics came to examine Drew. As they led him away, Chase turned to me and cupped my face with his hands.

"I wasn't sure how that was going to turn out for a minute," he said.

"Me neither. To think all those people died . . . for no good reason—other than selfishness," I muttered. "It seems like the ultimate act of iniquity."

"Unfortunately, there are a lot of those moments in life." He stepped back and took my hand in his. Gently, he rubbed my ring finger before planting a soft kiss there. "I'm never letting you out of my sight again. I hope you're okay with that."

A grin spread across my face. "I'm more than okay with that."

"Whatever the world throws at us . . . whatever friction might form between us when we feel passionate about something . . . as long as we decide to be in this together, we can make it work."

My heart turned into a puddle. "You're absolutely right. I love you, Chase. Always and forever."

"I love you too, Holly."

His lips met mine in a brief kiss, and for a moment everything around us disappeared. As we pulled away, I fell into his arms, glad I had a safe place to fall during those times when life was nearly too hard to comprehend.

It had been a long journey to get here, but things were finally balancing out. Chase and I could finally move on . . . together.

Life didn't always turn out the way you envisioned. But, when you were open to it, sometimes the detours ended up making the future even better than one could have ever expected.

EPILOGUE

I'D ALWAYS THOUGHT that spring was the perfect time for a wedding.

I'd also always thought that a traditional wedding in a beautiful church full of stained-glass windows was ideal. I wanted three bridesmaids, a dress with a long train, and roses. Lots of roses.

But more than that, I'd wanted the man of my dreams to be waiting at the end of that long aisle—the man of my dreams being someone who loved God, who loved me, and who loved others.

I'd found all of that in Chase.

I'd abandoned some of my fascination with all things old-fashioned, but not all of them. I'd started wearing my dresses again. I still loved baking, and making meals for people who were homebound, and even showing some of the teens in the neighborhood who were interested how to sew.

Some things couldn't be taken away from me—they'd only been temporarily put on pause.

After Olivia and Lars had been arrested, the police had found a video in their files. Indeed, they had set it up to look like Chase and I were responsible for everything that had happened. They'd even managed to use effects to make a grainy video that made it look like we'd killed Drew.

Thankfully, their plan hadn't worked. They'd be spending a long, long time behind bars.

I readjusted the bouquet in my hands as I stared nervously at the sanctuary. In a moment, I'd walk that aisle. Ralph would be at my side. Jamie, Alex, and Sarah would be going before me.

Sarah . . . who was now living back with her mom. We tried to get together once a week so I could still be a part of her life. I missed her terribly, but I was happy for her—happy that her little family had been restored.

Kari Leblanc was also here. Over the past six months, we'd taken strides in our relationship. She really was my cousin on my father's side. It would take a long time for me to be able to fully trust her, but I liked our progress so far. My family had also taken her in, and, in some way, I knew my father would be proud if he were here today.

Drew had even said he'd be here today. Our friendship had been able to continue, even though we weren't a couple. I'd even seen him and Kari talking a few times, and I suspected they'd come to the wedding together.

"You look stunning," Jamie said, pausing beside me in her wine-colored bridesmaid gown. Her own wedding was coming up in two months, so this would be great practice for her.

"Thank you."

"And I do believe that Chase is glowing up there on stage. I've never seen him look so happy before."

I grinned at her words. "That's great to know."

The song began playing, and Jamie gave me a quick kiss on the cheek. Then she started down the aisle behind the other bridesmaids.

I slipped my arm through Ralph's, and we waited our turn.

"Dad would be so proud of you right now, Holly," Ralph whispered. "You know that, right?"

I swallowed back tears. "Thanks, Ralph. I wish he could be here."

"We all do. At least we know he's not suffering anymore."

I thought he was going to take the breakup with Olivia hard, but he'd said he'd actually wanted to end things between them anyway. He seemed content to be by himself, waiting for the right woman to come along. And, if she didn't, Ralph seemed okay with that also.

As the music changed, I felt my cheeks flush. This

was it. This was my big moment.

Everyone rose as I stepped into the sanctuary. But I hardly noticed.

Mostly, I noticed Chase waiting for me.

It had been a long journey for us to get here, filled with a lot of twists and turns. But I had no doubt that this was what I wanted. That Chase was who I wanted.

After Ralph gave me away, I stepped up to Chase. He looked handsome in his classic black tux.

He leaned forward and kissed my cheek.

"Not yet," the minister joked.

Everyone laughed.

I handed my flowers to Jamie and took Chase's hands in mine.

The ceremony seemed to be both a blur and something that I'd always remember every single moment of.

Especially when the minister got to the end and said, "I now pronounce you husband and wife. You may kiss the bride."

Chase stepped toward me, his eyes filled with love. He drew me closer, and his lips covered mine—tastefully so.

But a million fireworks exploded in my head.

Chase and I . . . the fact that we were together wasn't by random chance. No, it was because God had brought two broken people together.

And I couldn't wait to spend the rest of my life with him. I'd do my best to stay out of trouble . . . maybe.

DEAR READER,

I hope you've enjoyed coming alongside me for Holly Anna's journey. I know I've enjoyed getting to know her and her friends.

The whole idea for this series started with a dream—a dream where someone broke into my house and cleaned it for me. The idea continued to grow from there, and eventually Holly Anna Paladin was born.

You may be asking if this is the last book in the series. The truth is that I hate ending a series. The characters all start feeling like real people to me, and wrapping up their stories is like closing the door on a long friendship.

But it's time for this series to at least take a break.

Let's not say goodbye for good; let's just say goodbye for now. Who knows when she might make another appearance in the future?

Much love,
Christy Barritt

ALSO BY CHRISTY BARRITT:

OTHER BOOKS IN THE HOLLY ANNA
PALADIN MYSTERIES:

When Holly Anna Paladin is given a year to live, she embraces her final days doing what she loves most—random acts of kindness. But when one of her extreme good deeds goes horribly wrong, implicating Holly in a string of murders, Holly is suddenly in a different kind of fight for her life. She knows one thing for sure: she only has a short amount of time to make a difference. And if helping the people she cares about puts her in danger, it's a risk worth taking.

#1 Random Acts of Murder

#2 Random Acts of Deceit

#2.5 Random Acts of Scrooge

#3 Random Acts of Malice

#4 Random Acts of Greed

YOU ALSO MIGHT ENJOY: THE LANTERN BEACH SERIES

LANTERN BEACH MYSTERIES

Hidden Currents

You can take the detective out of the investigation, but you can't take the investigator out of the detective. A notorious gang puts a bounty on Detective Cady Matthews's head after she takes down their leader, leaving her no choice but to hide until she can testify at trial. But her temporary home across the country on a remote North Carolina island isn't as peaceful as she initially thinks. Living under the new identity of Cassidy Livingston, she struggles to keep her investigative skills tucked away, especially after a body washes ashore. When local police bungle the murder investigation, she can't resist stepping in. But Cassidy is supposed to be keeping a low profile. One wrong move could lead to both her discovery and her demise. Can she bring justice to the island . . . or will the hidden currents surrounding her pull her under for good?

Flood Watch

The tide is high, and so is the danger on Lantern Beach. Still in hiding after infiltrating a dangerous gang, Cassidy Livingston just has to make it a few more months before she can testify at trial and resume her old life. But trouble keeps finding her, and Cassidy is pulled into a local investigation after a man mysteriously disappears from the island she now calls home. A recurring nightmare from her time undercover only muddies things, as does a visit from the parents of her handsome ex-Navy SEAL neighbor. When a friend's life is threatened, Cassidy must make choices that put her on the verge of blowing her cover. With a flood watch on her emotions and her life in a tangle, will Cassidy find the truth? Or will her past finally drown her?

Storm Surge

A storm is brewing hundreds of miles away, but its effects are devastating even from afar. Laid-back, loose, and light: that's Cassidy Livingston's new motto. But when a makeshift boat with a bloody cloth inside washes ashore near her oceanfront home, her detective instincts shift into gear . . . again. Seeking clues isn't the only thing on her mind—romance is heating up with next-door neighbor and former Navy SEAL Ty Chambers as well. Her heart wants the love and stability she's longed for her entire life. But her hidden identity only leads to a tidal wave of turbulence. As more answers emerge about the boat, the danger around her rises, creating a treacherous swell that threatens to reveal her past. Can Cassidy mind her own business, or will the storm surge of violence and corruption that has washed ashore on Lantern Beach leave her life in wreckage?

Dangerous Waters

Danger lurks on the horizon, leaving only two choices: find shelter or flee. Cassidy Livingston's new identity has begun to feel as comfortable as her favorite sweater. She's been tucked away on Lantern Beach for weeks, waiting to testify against a deadly gang, and is settling in to a new life she wants to last forever. When she thinks she spots someone malevolent from her past, panic swells inside her. If an enemy has found her, Cassidy won't be the only one who's a target. Everyone she's come to love will also be at risk. Dangerous waters threaten to pull her into an overpowering chasm she may never escape. Can Cassidy survive what lies ahead? Or has the tide fatally turned against her?

Perilous Riptide

Just when the current seems safer, an unseen danger emerges and threatens to destroy everything. When

Cassidy Livingston finds a journal hidden deep in the recesses of her ice cream truck, her curiosity kicks into high gear. Islanders suspect that Elsa, the journal's owner, didn't die accidentally. Her final entry indicates their suspicions might be correct and that what Elsa observed on her final night may have led to her demise. Against the advice of Ty Chambers, her former Navy SEAL boyfriend, Cassidy taps into her detective skills and hunts for answers. But her search only leads to a skeletal body and trouble for both of them. As helplessness threatens to drown her, Cassidy is desperate to turn back time. Can Cassidy find what she needs to navigate the perilous situation? Or will the riptide surrounding her threaten everyone and everything Cassidy loves?

Deadly Undertow

The current's fatal pull is powerful, but so is one detective's will to live. When someone from Cassidy Livingston's past shows up on Lantern Beach and warns her of impending peril, opposing currents collide, threatening to drag her under. Running would be easy. But leaving would break her heart. Cassidy must decipher between the truth and lies, between reality and deception. Even more importantly, she must decide whom to trust and whom to fear. Her life depends on it. As danger rises and answers surface, everything Cassidy thought she knew is tested. In order to survive, Cassidy must take drastic measures and end the battle against the ruthless gang DH-7 once and for all. But if her final mission fails, the consequences will be as deadly as the raging undertow.

LANTERN BEACH ROMANTIC SUSPENSE

Tides of Deception

Change has come to Lantern Beach: a new police chief, a new season, and . . . a new romance? Austin Brooks has loved Skye Lavinia from the moment they met, but the walls she keeps around her seem impenetrable. Skye knows Austin is the best thing to ever happen to her. Yet she also knows that if he learns the truth about her past, he'd be a fool not to run. A chance encounter brings secrets bubbling to the surface, and danger soon follows. Are the life-threatening events plaguing them really accidents . . . or is someone trying to send a deadly message? With the tides on Lantern Beach come deception and lies. One question remains— who will be swept away as the water shifts? And will it bring the end for Austin and Skye, or merely the beginning?

Shadow of Intrigue

For her entire life, Lisa Garth has felt like a supporting character in the drama of life. The designation never bothered her—until now. Lantern Beach, where she's settled and runs a popular restaurant, has boarded up for the season. The slower pace leaves her with too much time alone. Braden Dillinger came to Lantern Beach to try to heal. The former Special Forces officer returned from battle with invisible scars and diminished hope. But his recovery is hampered by the fact that an unknown enemy is trying to kill him. From the moment Lisa and Braden meet, danger ignites around them, and both are drawn into a web of intrigue that turns their lives upside down. As shadows creep in, will Lisa and Braden be able to shine a light on the peril around them? Or will the encroaching darkness turn their worst nightmares into reality?

Storm of Doubt

A pastor who's lost faith in God. A romance writer who's lost faith in love. A faceless man with a deadly obsession. Nothing has felt right in Pastor Jack Wilson's world since his wife died two years ago. He hoped coming to Lantern Beach might help soothe the ragged edges of his soul. Instead, he feels more alone than ever. Novelist Juliette Grace came to the island to hide away. Though her professional life has never been better, her personal life has imploded. Her husband left her and a stalker's threats have grown more and more dangerous. When Jack saves Juliette from an attack, he sees the terror in her gaze and knows he must protect her. But when danger strikes again, will Jack be able to keep her safe? Or will the approaching storm prove too strong to withstand?

LANTERN BEACH PD

On the Lookout

When Cassidy Chambers accepted the job as police chief on Lantern Beach, she knew the island had its secrets. But a suspicious death with potentially far-reaching implications will test all her skills—and threaten to reveal her true identity. Cassidy enlists the help of her husband, former Navy SEAL Ty Chambers. As they dig for answers, both uncover parts of their pasts that are best left buried. Not everything is as it seems, and they must figure out if their John Doe is connected to the secretive group that has moved onto the island. As facts materialize, danger on the island grows. Can Cassidy and Ty discover the truth about the shadowy crimes in their cozy community? Or has darkness permanently invaded their beloved Lantern Beach?

Attempt to Locate

A fun girls' night out turns into a nightmare when armed robbers barge into the store where Cassidy and her friends are shopping. As the situation escalates and the men escape, a massive manhunt launches on Lantern Beach to apprehend the dangerous trio. In the midst of the chaos, a potential foe asks for Cassidy's help. He needs to find his sister who fled from the secretive Gilead's Cove community on the island. But the more Cassidy learns about the seemingly untouchable group, the more her unease grows. The pressure to solve both cases continues to mount. But as the gravity of the situation rises, so does the danger. Cassidy is determined to protect the island and break up the cult . . . but doing so might cost her everything.

First Degree Murder

Police Chief Cassidy Chambers longs for a break from the recent crimes plaguing Lantern Beach. She simply wants to enjoy her friends' upcoming wedding, to prepare for the busy tourist season about to slam the island, and to gather all the dirt she can on the suspicious community that's invaded the town. But trouble explodes on the island, sending residents—including Cassidy—into a squall of uneasiness. Cassidy may have more than one enemy plotting her demise, and the collateral damage seems unthinkable. As the temperature rises, so does the pressure to find answers. Someone is determined that Lantern Beach would be better off without their new police chief. And for Cassidy, one wrong move could mean certain death.

Dead on Arrival

With a highly charged local election consuming the community, Police Chief Cassidy Chambers braces herself for a challenging day of breaking up petty conflicts and tamping down high emotions. But when widespread food poisoning spreads among potential voters across the island, Cassidy smells something rotten in the air. As Cassidy examines every possibility to uncover what's going on, local enigma Anthony Gilead again comes on her radar. The man is running for mayor and his cult-like following is growing at an alarming rate. Cassidy feels certain he has a spy embedded in her inner circle. The problem is that her pool of suspects gets deeper every day. Can Cassidy get to the bottom of what's eating away at her peaceful island home? Will voters turn out despite the outbreak of illness plaguing their tranquil town? And the even bigger question: Has darkness come to stay on Lantern Beach?

THE WORST DETECTIVE EVER:

I'm not really a private detective. I just play one on TV.

Joey Darling, better known to the world as Raven Remington, detective extraordinaire, is trying to separate herself from her invincible alter ego. She played the spunky character for five years on the hit TV show *Relentless*, which catapulted her to fame and into the role of Hollywood's sweetheart. When her marriage falls apart, her finances dwindle to nothing, and her father disappears, Joey finds herself on the Outer Banks of North Carolina, trying to piece together her life away from the limelight. But as people continually mistake her for the character she played on TV, she's tasked with solving real life crimes . . . even though she's terrible at it.

ABOUT THE AUTHOR

USA Today has called Christy Barritt's books "scary, funny, passionate, and quirky."

Christy writes both mystery and romantic suspense novels that are clean with underlying messages of faith. Her books have won the Daphne du Maurier Award for Excellence in Suspense and Mystery, have been twice nominated for the Romantic Times Reviewers' Choice Award, and have finaled for both a Carol Award and Foreword Magazine's Book of the Year.

She is married to her Prince Charming, a man who thinks she's hilarious—but only when she's not trying to be. Christy is a self-proclaimed klutz, an avid music lover who's known for spontaneously bursting into song, and a road trip aficionado.

When she's not working or spending time with her family, she enjoys singing, playing the guitar, and exploring small, unsuspecting towns where people have no idea how accident-prone she is.

Find Christy online at:

www.christybarritt.com
www.facebook.com/christybarritt
www.twitter.com/cbarritt

Sign up for Christy's newsletter to get information on all of her latest releases here: **www.christybarritt.com/newsletter-sign-up/**

If you enjoyed this book, please consider leaving a review.

Made in the USA
Middletown, DE
28 August 2019